little fur
A Fox Called Sorrow

BOOKS BY ISOBELLE CARMODY

Little Fur

The Legend Begins

A Fox Called Sorrow

The Gateway Trilogy

Night Gate

Winter Door

The Fire Cat (2008)

The Obernewtyn Chronicles

Obernewtyn

The Farseekers

Ashling

The Keeping Place

little fur

Book 2

A Fox Called Sorrow

ISOBELLE CARMODY

RANDOM HOUSE  NEW YORK

For my elfin girl

Copyright © 2006 by Isobelle Carmody

Published in the United States by Random House Children's Books,
a division of Random House, Inc., New York. Originally published in Australia as
The Legend of Little Fur, Book 2, A Fox Called Sorrow by Viking,
an imprint of Penguin Books Australia, Camberwell, in 2006.

RANDOM HOUSE and colophon are registered trademarks of Random House, Inc.

www.randomhouse.com/kids

Educators and librarians, for a variety of teaching tools, visit us at
www.randomhouse.com/teachers

Library of Congress Cataloging-in-Publication Data
Carmody, Isobelle.
A fox called Sorrow / Isobelle Carmody. — 1st American ed.
p.   cm. — (Little Fur ; bk. 2)
SUMMARY: On a dangerous quest to the troll city of Underth, the healer,
Little Fur, is mystified by a new companion—a scarred and angry fox
whose strong spirit keeps him alive despite his wish to die.
ISBN: 978-0-375-83856-9 (trade) — ISBN: 978-0-375-93856-6 (lib. bdg.) —
ISBN: 978-0-375-83857-6 (pbk.)
[1. Elves—Fiction. 2. Adventure and adventurers—Fiction.
3. Animals—Fiction. 4. Fantasy.]
I. Title. II. Series: Carmody, Isobelle. Little Fur ; bk. 2.
PZ7.C2176Fo 2007 [Fic]—dc22 2006011816

Design by Marina Messiha

PRINTED IN CHINA

10 9 8 7 6 5 4 3 2 1

First American Edition

CONTENTS

CHAPTER 1

A Storm of Omens

It was autumn, and as sometimes happens in that season of heavy golden light and falling leaves, a powerful storm began to brew itself. It sucked up secrets and hidden purposes like leaves, flinging them into the air as omens.

Humans, blind and deaf to all but their own desires, could not easily read such signs. But as the storm gathered, children tossed in their beds and threw up an arm as if to ward off a blow. Hidden in the shadows, greeps, once humans whose strange, dreadful appetites had dimmed

1

their minds and twisted their bodies, had a blurred awareness that something bad was coming. But they felt only an ugly pleasure at the thought that someone might suffer.

Wild creatures living within the city, and even some of the tame beasts dwelling with humans, sensed the warnings that churned in the air. But most of the animals responded with no more than a surge of instinct. Squirrels rushed to check their secret hoards, and rabbits examined the roofs of their burrows; ants rushed hither and thither; birds fortified their nests and turned their eggs anxiously.

A dog chained in a bare stone yard sensed the rage and hatred in the omens. Half insane from thirst and mistreatment, she began pulling ferociously at her bonds, ignoring the chafing of the collar fastened about her neck.

In the city zoo, a lion roared and would not be soothed no matter how much bloody meat its keeper gave it, and two panthers wove about each other in a tapestry of apprehension. In another enclosure, a frenzy of monkeys mimicked the violence they scented in the wind.

A half-starved fox limped toward the outskirts of the sprawling gray city over which the storm spread its black and ragged wings. He stopped to sniff at the wind and to read the warnings and signals. But his anguish was so great that if the world were to end he would not have minded. He limped on.

Those few creatures left over from a previous age could read the omens clearly, for they had been born when all honored the wind, knowing it for a great herald. But such omens required brooding upon to be properly understood.

A pixie who lived at the edge of the inland city over which the storm churned paused in the grooming of his beloved tree to stare at the clouds. He was troubled by the knowledge that by morning the russet glory of its leaves would be torn away. But the roots of the tree ran deep and there would be new leaves in the spring. He touched the leaves tenderly, turning his back on the clouds and their omens.

A boil of trolls at the mouth of a pipe leaking poisonous filth saw a lurid slash of light along the underside of the bruised-looking clouds and fell to hissing and cackling in delight.

Only one being sought to unravel the signs. Not a creature from a past age of the world, but a crippled, raggedy owl who dwelt in a church that the animals thought of as a beaked house. This was no ordinary church. Raised at the very cusp of the last age, it was a place where humans had brought hope for hundreds of years. So powerful was the accumulation of their longing that a still and potent magic had pooled there. The owl, who had retreated, wounded, to this church many years before, was saturated in it.

The storm rattled the shingles on the steeple and ancient beams began to strain and warp. The owl tilted her head and listened. She watched the stained-glass windows flash with daggers of

storm light. Gradually the Sett Owl understood. *The vital earth spirit, which seeks to unite all living things just as a mother strives for peace among her children, will soon face a terrible danger.* The owl was not surprised to discover that the Troll King lay behind the threat. But try as she might, she could not discover what form the threat would take.

The magic within the Sett Owl allowed her to commune with the earth spirit. The owl learned more of the darkness that loomed, but little of what might be done to prevent it. Yet the earth spirit offered the fragile and unimaginably sweet scent of hope, not only for the world, or for this city where trees once sang, but for the owl herself, too.

The Sett Owl was very old, even among her long-lived kind. She desired to pass from life and join the world's dream, but the still magic of the church would not permit it. The owl had to wait until one came who would take her place.

There was a loud crack of thunder. The earth

magic that flowed about the old church surged. The Sett Owl had a clear, bright vision of the elf troll Little Fur. Small as a three-year-old human, with pointed ears and brambling red hair, the gentle healer dwelt in a secret wilderness within the city that was hidden from human eyes by seven magical trees. Little Fur had once gone on a perilous quest to protect those ancient trees, whom she called the Old Ones.

At first the Sett Owl thought the vision meant that Little Fur must again sally forth. Then she realized that the elf troll was not the *answer* to the danger foretold by the storm, but the *reason* for the Troll King's plotting. The owl considered summoning the healer, but what could she say to her? It was not as if Little Fur had done anything wrong. Indeed, the opposite was true.

The Sett Owl did not question the earth spirit further because, where the elf troll was concerned, the earth spirit made no predictions. Perhaps it was because her parents had been a troll and an elf. But whatever the reason, Little Fur possessed a quality that was truly strange: she was *random*.

The Sett Owl gave a wheezy sigh and wished that these matters might have waited for her successor, but it was not to be. Well, the earth spirit had urged her to seek knowledge. If she could amass enough small pieces of information, perhaps she would get a clearer picture of what the Troll King planned.

Not far away, the storm front approached the hidden wilderness, but Little Fur did not notice the darkening sky, let alone the omens and signs driven before the storm. She was absorbed in trying to remove a grass seed from the badly infected paw of a raccoon. Two rabbits, a mouse, three birds and a hedgehog awaited her attention, and her stomach was rumbling with hunger, for she had eaten nothing since the morning.

Little Fur was concentrating so hard that she did not notice the rain beginning to fall, or its strange bitter taste. She had managed to work the grass seed out and was gently rubbing in salve to treat the infection when the drops of rain began to fall with a force that scattered her remaining patients. Little Fur scooped up the raccoon and retreated under the branches of the nearest tree. In the spring, the tree's thick foliage would have provided good cover, but it was autumn and its few remaining leaves were being harvested by the rising wind and slashing rain.

If alone, Little Fur would have hurried through the rain to the hill that rose behind her, pushed through the crown of brambles at the top and dashed down the steep winding track into the valley where the Old Ones grew. Beneath their dense, magical canopy, she would be safe from any storm. But the raccoon was too heavy to carry far and she could not leave her. Little Fur knew, as any true healer does, that mending the flesh is only half the task of healing a wound or sickness. Carrying the raccoon carefully, she picked her way between the trees, staying under cover as best she could until she reached a hollow tree. She climbed into its belly and began to croon a song to the raccoon's spirit.

Gazing out at the sky as she sang, Little Fur noticed black thunderheads rising like phantom mountains above the trees. Lightning lashed across the sky, illuminating the distant human

high houses. The shining towers showed no sign of bending before the storm; only things that were alive had the sense to bow before such a force. The high houses looked impervious, whereas all about her the trees bent and creaked and lashed their branches. Yet Little Fur knew it would be the city that suffered the greatest damage. Many of the small animals and birds that lived there would be hurt and would come to the wilderness seeking her healing skills.

There would be injuries within the wilderness as well. Nothing serious, Little Fur hoped, for she did not like to imagine that life and death might flutter under her hands; it was too great a responsibility. Such matters ought to be brought only before noble creatures like the Old Ones or the Sett Owl. An unease crept into her bones, but she dismissed it, telling herself she must rest and prepare for the days to come.

Little Fur's thoughts drifted back to the high houses. She wondered if some human was also staring out at the storm, and whether it was fearful or unafraid. Once Little Fur could not have imagined that creatures as malevolent and violent as humans could fear anything. But she had learned through her first, perilous journey into the city—and the many forays she had made afterward to plant seeds—that humans were as different from one another as the creatures of any other species.

Humans *were* dangerous, though. To remind herself of that, Little Fur had only to think of the animals she had healed whose injuries had been caused by humans. But she now knew that rather than being essentially evil, humans harmed and destroyed from fear or confusion, or even by accident, as much as from a love of violence. She had smelled their cruelty and hatred and anger, but she also had caught the delicious scent of human curiosity and heard the astonishing beauty and power of human song. What she felt now about humans was a mixture of inquisitiveness and wariness.

Little Fur had decided that humans were the way they were because they did not feel the flow of the earth magic, which joined all living things. Every time she planted a new seed, it would summon the earth spirit; Little Fur thought that if she could just plant enough seeds, the earth spirit would flow so strongly through the city that humans could not help but feel it. Then they would cease to trollishly loathe and despoil nature.

Little Fur knew that in a way, she was trying to heal humankind. The ambition made her want to laugh. She was so small and the city so large. Yet each time she set out into the streets, she could feel that her plantings were making a difference. The earth magic *was* flowing more strongly there than when she had first stepped out of the wilderness.

Little Fur curled around the sleeping raccoon and drowsed. Occasionally she opened her eyes to see the curtain of rain sway aside, offering a glimpse of the high houses. Sometimes the gleaming surfaces reflected the jagged lightning, making it look as if they had cracked like sheets of ice.

It was not until near morning that Little Fur slept properly. Shreds of storm omens followed her into sleep. She dreamed she was crawling through cramped, dank tunnels under the earth. She could hear the shriek of wind and the low, urgent growl of thunder, but it came from below rather than above, as if a great storm churned at the heart of the world. Little Fur was trying to find her way to it so that she could plant a seed that would heal its hurt. Then she realized she had lost her seed pouch. . . .

Little Fur woke to a dazzle of light and the elated song of a thrush bubbling out into the new day.

CHAPTER 2
Healing the Sick

Little Fur roused herself and found that the raccoon had become tangled in her tunic. She climbed out of the tree and set the raccoon down, accepting her thanks with a smile.

Looking around, she saw that the storm *had* wreaked havoc, but nothing permanent. If a tree had fallen down in the wilderness, she would have known it, for the earth spirit always carried such tidings. The worst damage was to a tree that had been split by a bolt of lightning, but it would live, as long as Little Fur kept the black rot from entering its heart. Other than that, the storm had mostly hastened the stripping of the trees. Even so, a surprising number of ruddy leaves clung gamely to their branches.

A screeched greeting interrupted Little Fur's observations. She smiled up at Crow, who was one of her best friends.

"Craaak! You not coming to Old Ones last night," Crow scolded, landing on a low branch so that he could glare at her properly. "They are full of angriness."

Little Fur laughed, coming to stroke his gleaming black feathers. "What a bad bird you are to tell such lies. Trees do not feel anger."

"They missing you," he amended sullenly.

"But we were not truly apart, for the flow of earth magic connected us," Little Fur said.

Crow gave a rather rude caw and launched himself into the air in the direction of the hill meadow where Little Fur treated most of her patients. Little Fur smiled, knowing he would announce her arrival. Crow loved heralding her, and fortunately, he had ceased to recount their adventures. His stories had become so outrageously exaggerated that even the most gullible birds and rabbits ended up refusing to believe "the Legend of Little Fur," as he called it.

As Little Fur pushed through the wet grass and foliage, she noted the trees that would need attention. Arriving at the hill meadow, she saw that there were no patients and no Crow. No doubt he had flown off when he had found no audience. She washed her face in the silvery ribbon of a stream that sprang out of the side of the hill and ran across the meadow. Then she

sat and dangled her feet over the edge, where the stream tumbled into a frothing fall of water.

"Excuse me, Healer, there is something you should see." It was Tillet, her most consistent and useful helper.

Little Fur smiled at the hare and rose. She did

not ask where they were going, because the hare did not like to speak except when it was absolutely necessary. This quality made her a competent and restful assistant, unlike Little Fur's other helpers, the chattering squirrels and rabbits. Little Fur wondered why Tillet chose to help her, but if asked, the rangy hare would undoubtedly have asked Little Fur why she healed. And what was the answer? Little Fur could heal and so she did. It was as simple as that.

Tillet stopped by a weed-choked crevice in a tumble of rocks in the place where the meadow sprang out from the hill. After one swift glance back, the hare bounded into it. Upon entering, Little Fur found that the cranny widened into an open space. Tillet was standing beside a flowering plant that usually bloomed only in the spring, and whose seeds were wonderful at lowering fevers. If it could be kept alive this late every year, Little Fur need never run short again! She harvested the seeds and then planted a few

nearby, singing a song to the earth spirit to ask that it welcome and nurture them.

Little Fur and Tillet had just emerged from the crevice when a lively little squirrel came chittering up to announce that Little Fur's first patient had arrived. They followed his bobbing tail back to the hill meadow, where a fat, depressed-looking frog sat on a flat stone by the side of the stream.

"What is the matter?" Little Fur asked.

The frog explained hoarsely that he had accidentally swallowed a bee. He opened his mouth and Little Fur grimaced at his swollen throat. Luckily, it was not blocking the windpipe, or the poor frog would have suffocated! She pulled out the stinger, then made a tisane from stream water and herbs in a wooden bowl, sweetening it with berry juice. She set the bowl down in front of the frog, and he gulped the tisane down mournfully before thanking her and hopping away.

Her next patient was a beautiful white rabbit, who had escaped from her human owner during the storm.

"I did come like a bird from an egg," the rabbit cried, wild-eyed and amazed by her own courage. As she had escaped, the rabbit had gashed herself on a jagged bit of metal. Little Fur could smell a slight scent of infection about the wound, but luckily, the rabbit had come to her quickly.

Little Fur carefully cleaned the cut as the rabbit told her breath-lessly how a cow had advised her to seek out an enchanted wilderness within the city, where a beautiful fairy would heal her wounds. "You do not look much like a fairy," the rabbit added doubtfully.

Little Fur hid a smile. "That is because I am not a fairy." She ground a few potent seeds to fight the infection and mixed them with a honey salve, marveling at the funny ideas creatures had about her.

"Thank you, Your Majesty," the white rabbit whispered when Little Fur had finished.

She turned her attention to her next patient, a mole with a rash. Then came a big rude hawk, who cursed Little Fur's clumsiness as she applied salve to her torn wing. When Little Fur was done, the hawk flew away without a word of thanks, and Little Fur heard Tillet sigh in vexation.

"I do not heal in order that my patients will admire me or bow to me," Little Fur told the hare. "Hawks are highly strung, and the tear in her wing was very deep, yet she did not cry out once."

"A little gratitude never hurt," Tillet said tartly.

Next came a big tomcat, whose baleful glare made all the rabbits vanish and upset a number of other small creatures waiting to be healed. Only Tillet showed no fear, and Little Fur wondered at her constancy. Little Fur had treated the tom before; he lived in one of the human houses close to the wilderness. The tom's eye was scratched, and examining it, Little Fur sighed.

"Why do cats fight so much?" she asked.

"It is a matter of territory," he said mildly. Despite his squashed face and glaring eyes, he was not a bad-tempered cat.

"Not *all* cats fight," Little Fur said.

"Cats that do not fight are unnatural," the cat countered, wincing as she lifted his eyelid.

Little Fur said nothing. She was thinking of other cats she knew. "That is the best I can do," she told the tomcat when she had completed her tending. "I am not sure that it will heal properly. Perhaps you had better come again soon."

The cat agreed languidly, but Little Fur could smell that he was not listening to her. Well, she could not make him come, and perhaps the eye would heal cleanly.

Crow did not make another appearance until the sun was high overhead. Little Fur had washed her hands and was nibbling on some nuts from the squirrels when Crow landed beside her, fluffing himself up and rustling his feathers importantly.

"Storm doing much damaging," he began.

"No trees fell, and what was crushed or flooded will grow again," Little Fur said.

"High houses flooded and some bits of them broken off and breaking other dwellings. Sky-fire burning some low houses," Crow said, to make clear that he had been flying over the city.

"The humans will rebuild," Little Fur said. Humans were constantly pulling down bits of the city to build them anew.

Having eaten the nuts, Little Fur went to see to her next patient, a seagull who had been dashed into the side of one of the high houses. The lower part of his beak was cracked, and Crow hippity-hopped over to watch as Little Fur pounded a lump of dried tree sap into powder. She added certain seeds and mixed everything together with water to form a strong glue. The crack was small, but it was better to fix it, so that it could not catch on anything.

"You are far from the sea," Little Fur murmured as she waited for the glue to reach the right consistency.

"Cah! Wind catching me . . . from the storming," the gull said. His words were even more scattered than other birds', since his mind was full of winds and strange currents.

Little Fur did not say anything else, because she needed the bird to keep his beak still. She held the beak firmly, sensing that the bird was distracted by a late butterfly dancing in the air. There was no point in scolding, because unlike

Crow, who could force himself to concentrate, the seagull was incapable of remembering anything for more than a few moments.

Little Fur was sorry that another great friend, Brownie, was not here. He could have held the bird's attention by talking about waves. The pony had been born by the sea, and from time to time he returned there with his brothers and his human owner. "You must hold your beak open until the glue sets," Little Fur told the seagull, and carefully put a pebble into the bottom part of his beak. "This will make sure you do not get the bottom of your beak stuck to the top."

"What if the beak sticks to the stone?" Crow asked. The gull gave him a wild sideways glare.

"The stone is coated in dried glue, which is the

only thing the wet glue won't stick to. Now just sit quietly. It won't take long to dry."

It was then that Ginger the cat appeared.

The seagull hopped sideways in agitation, but Little Fur insisted there was no danger. "Can't you smell that he won't hurt you?" she asked.

The seagull muttered indistinctly that the stink of the glue was too strong for him to smell anything else, but he was reassured by Crow's lack of fear. Little Fur turned to greet Ginger properly, but before she could say a word, the gray cat spat out a sodden clod of mud and feathers.

The clod shuddered. It was a baby owl so young that she had only a few downy feathers. Her enormous yellow eyes blinked blindly in the brightness. She uttered a soft *whoo*, then rolled over in a swoon!

CHAPTER 3
Out of the Wilderness

Little Fur carried the baby owl to a nearby evergreen tree.

"If I had left it cheeping where it was, a cat would have eaten it," Ginger remarked, padding silently beside Little Fur.

"The Old Ones would not have let harm come to something that needed healing," Little Fur assured him as she cleaned and dried the tiny bird, who hardly seemed to know what was happening to her.

Little Fur had a bird bring worms, but the

owlet barely touched them. In the end, Little Fur put her in a nest that she kept prepared.

"Can you remember where you found the owlet?" Little Fur asked Ginger.

"I found her on the ground beside a broken human high house. Road monsters had been gnawing at the buildings," Ginger said.

Little Fur stared. Ginger had *not* found the owlet in the wilderness, as she had supposed, but in the city, where the cat might have made a meal of it. Instead, he had carried the owlet to her in his mouth. Truly, he was unlike other cats!

Little Fur turned to Crow. "*Dear* Crow," she began, knowing how difficult he could be, "would you fly to the city and tell the owls that a nestling has been found and is safe in the wilderness?"

For all her tact, Crow refused. "Owls hating crows because flock attacking Sett Owl when she being fledgling!" he said.

"That was a very long time ago," Little Fur insisted. "Just think, when she grows up, she will tell all of the other owls about the brave and heroic crow who helped her to return to her family."

But Crow was too much the master of such exaggerations himself to be swayed by Little Fur's attempt. In exasperation, she summoned a starling. There was no use in giving the bird a complicated message, so she merely asked it to spread the news about the owlet. The day passed without any sign of an owl, and Little Fur guessed that the starling had probably forgotten her request. Checking on the owlet later in the day, Little Fur smelled that its tiny battered body was neither infected nor feverish, but she could detect the ominous scents of loneliness and neglect that came with the loss of a mother.

Little Fur wondered what to do. If she asked another bird to deliver a message to the owls, the result would likely be the same as with the starling. The bird would forget to deliver the message or muddle it so badly that no sense could be made of it. That was how birds were—except Crow, whose powerful curiosity and extravagant imagination helped him think more clearly. He was the only bird other than an owl capable of carrying messages. But there was no point in asking him when he had already refused.

The unease Little Fur had felt the night before was now stronger. The time had come to make another journey into the city. The thought of leaving the wilderness filled her with worry. She couldn't get used to the smell of the roads that ran like veins through the human city, or the dreadful road beasts that prowled them day and night. And apart from the humans, there were trolls that roamed the city after dark and, of course, greeps. Worst of all, something might force her to break contact with the flow of earth magic. If that happened, she knew she would be severed from it forever.

But the owlet needed her mother, and Little Fur saw no other way to help her.

It was near dusk, the blue sky filled with delicate feathers of pink and gold, when Little Fur told

Tillet of her decision. Tillet shook her long ears and bounded away to get the spare seed pouch she kept in her burrow for Little Fur.

"Be careful" was all Tillet said as she watched Little Fur sling the extra pouch over her shoulder to hang beside the one she always carried.

Crow was less moderate.

"Craaak! This being the stupidest idea that was ever thinked!" he screeched. "City is being flooded! Too much raining. Buildings has been falling down. Terrible sickness is in city. Everyone dying!"

"It's a sickness among cats," Little Fur said calmly, for she had heard of it. "And this will be a good chance to examine a sick cat to see if there is something I can do to help." So far,

32

she had seen nothing of the sick cats. The reports of a cat epidemic had come from cats like the tom. "I am a healer, after all," she added when it looked like Crow was about to start screeching again. "Now I am leaving for the city. Do you want to come?"

He glowered at her and flapped off in a huff. Little Fur smiled, knowing that he would be waiting for her at the edge of the wilderness, as would Ginger. Little Fur put on a cloak made of a bit of human cloth that had been blown into the wilderness. She thought of the spiderweb cloak from her elf father, which had the marvelous property of weaving a grayness that made its wearer almost invisible. The last time she had seen the cloak it had been in the hand of an enormous cruel-smelling human who had tried to capture her.

Little Fur's last task before she left was to check on the baby owl, who was being watched over by two squirrels. The squirrels whispered that the owlet was sleeping, proof of the tiny bird's bewilderment, for she ought to have been waking for the night. And no wonder the poor little thing was deeply confused—few birds had the experience of being thrown out of their nest in a violent storm, then carried around inside the mouth of a cat!

Little Fur laid her hands on the evergreen tree in which the nest sat, and sang a plea to the earth spirit to watch over the owlet. She felt the whisper of earth magic through the tree and under her bare feet, reassuring her that the owl would come to no harm. She sent her thanks into the tree, along with a message of love and farewell to the Old Ones.

At last, Little Fur set off for the outer edge of the wilderness. She reminded herself to keep her feet—or some part of her—on the ground. If she lost contact with the flow of earth magic, even for a moment, she would not be able to return to the magical wilderness. She deliberately frightened herself with this thought in order to make sure she was properly careful.

Little Fur pushed through the voracious creeper that knitted all of the trees and bushes around the wilderness into a nearly impassable wall of green. She came out in a place where fields stretched away to distant fences. Beyond were rows of low human dwellings.

Little Fur's feet sank deep into the rain-soaked earth as she crossed the fields, heading for a lane between the low buildings. Once in the lane, she could hear the muted sounds of humans going about their affairs. She was not afraid, because none of the dwellings opened onto the lane. Nevertheless, she was careful, for there was always the danger that a greep might be in the shadow of one of the trees. Having been captured by one once, she was always alert for their rotted-fruit smell.

Ginger was waiting near the end of the lane. Behind him lay three black roads that had to be crossed before they could reach the beaked house where the Sett Owl lived. Little Fur had come this way many times, but the ugliness and stench

of the black roads always made her feel sick. She had just stepped onto the grass path between the road and the fence that bordered it when Crow appeared with his harsh cry of greeting. He landed on a peg that jutted from one of the tall wooden poles that humans planted along the black roads. These poles were connected by long thin lines of metal that sometimes sang eerie mindless tunes in the wind and at other times gave off sparks of sky-fire.

"Where we going firstness?" Crow asked as if he had never opposed the journey.

"The beaked house where the Sett Owl lives," Little Fur said. "While I speak to her, you can look for new places for me to plant seeds on the way back."

She set off at a trot along the verge. It was not long before the grass narrowed to a seam poking up along a path beside the wooden fence by the edge of the road. The path was human-made of the hard gray stuff which her friend Brownie called cement. (Being a pony who lived with humans, he knew a great deal about them.)

Little Fur carefully followed the seam of grass, knowing that it would widen again. Soon they approached the pipe Little Fur used as a tunnel under the black roads. Tonight the hollow where it emerged brimmed with muddy gray storm water.

"Maybe there is another pipe," Ginger murmured.

"Faraway is being other pipe," Crow muttered.

Little Fur sighed. There was enough of a gap between the top of the pipe and the swirling surface of the water for her to get through, but the water was so deep that she would have to swim. She took off her two seed pouches and slung them around Ginger's neck. Then she drew a deep breath and stepped into the water. It was very cold, and the earth magic in it was thin because of the poisons the rain had washed from the road. She gritted her teeth and went deeper.

Little Fur did not look back to see if Ginger was waiting, for her senses told her that he was already crossing the road. Being an animal, and a creature born in this age of the world, he would not be harmed if he lost touch with the flow of magic for a while. But she willed him to make haste, because crossing a black road was very dangerous. Road beasts raced along them at terrible speeds, and their glaring eyes were as hypnotic as a snake's. Of course, Ginger was used to crossing black roads, but Little Fur was always glad when this part of the journey was over. Crow was in no danger, naturally, because he could fly.

The tunnel widened, but in flattening out it left less space for breathing. Little Fur had to lie on her back to keep her mouth above water. Fortunately, a slight current carried her along. By the time she reached the end of the pipe, her neck ached from holding her chin up, and she was shivering with cold. Ginger had to help her from the water with his teeth and claws. He offered to lick her dry, but she refused, saying she would warm up soon enough.

They set off again, going back the way they had come. The grassy seam was thicker than on her last visit. Little Fur was pleased that some of the seeds she had planted on the other side of the black road had blown here and taken root, drawing the flow of earth magic and strengthening the grasses.

CHAPTER 4
The Beaked House

Little Fur smelled the road-beast feeding place long before they reached it. Where the fence angled back, she peeped out at the bright, flat-roofed house with its strange metal wings held motionless on either side. Dazzling streams of false light flowed out into the darkness, for its walls were made of the unmelting ice humans made. A smaller black road curved in from the bigger one to pass under the metal wings of the bright house. Two giant road beasts sat under the wings, letting humans tend to them. After

41

some time, they roared to life and sped away. One large road monster remained, but it looked soundly asleep.

"They will not see you," Ginger murmured, so gently that Little Fur guessed he could smell her fear. "The false light dazzles them."

She gathered her courage and stepped out onto the stubble of grass that ran along the fence. The rest of the ground was covered with cement. They had almost reached a gap in the fence when Little Fur saw a human sitting with its back to the fence.

"Don't worry," Ginger said, and slipped by her.

Little Fur's heart was in her throat as the cat approached the seated human. The human noticed Ginger and reached out to stroke him. Little Fur began to move, step by careful step, toward the gap in the fence. Soon she was close enough that the human had only to turn its head to see her, close enough to smell and be smelled, but its attention was completely focused on

Ginger. Little Fur smelled its longing to take him home.

Reaching the opening safely, she stepped through, making sure that she could feel the flow of earth magic before she lifted her back foot. She went a little distance from the gap and sat down to wait for Ginger, wondering why humans always wanted to own what pleased them. When Ginger leaped over the fence, Little Fur got up and they set off again across another field.

"The human smelled sad," she said.

"It smelled of too much being alone," Ginger answered. "Many humans do not like being alone. It is one of the things that can turn them into greeps."

"Maybe that is why the human smelled of wanting to keep you."

"Humans think nothing will stay with them unless it must," Ginger said.

Little Fur pondered this until they came to the stand of pear trees at one corner of the field they had crossed. Some goats were moving around

under the trees and the nearest came trotting
over. Little Fur could smell the reek of humans
over its strong musky scent, and the distinct
smell of wildness that all young things gave off.
She offered her hand and the kid sniffed it.

"You smell of troll," said the kid.

"I have troll blood in me," Little Fur admitted, "but I am not a troll."

The kid snorted. "Once trolls tried to catch me. They smelled of hunger and deadliness and hate." She gave a snicker of laughter. "My mother tells me that I must be afraid, because fear will help me to run faster. But I can run fast without being afraid."

Little Fur wondered if the kid was telling the truth. Usually, trolls loathed the rich flow of earth magic summoned by growing things. Yet the kid did not smell of lies or even of exaggeration.

As if she sensed Little Fur's thought, the kid said, "When my horns are long, I will escape from this stupid flat place and climb up to the clouds. My mother says that all the world is flat, and humans are the masters of it. But I dream of going up and up, to where there are no human masters, and the dream burns me, so that I know it is true."

"In the wilderness where I live, there are no humans," Little Fur said. "But you would have to cross black roads to reach it."

"Does the ground go up to the sky there?" the kid asked.

"Not to the sky, but—"

The kid cut her off scornfully. "Then I will not come." She gave Little Fur another close look. "What has troll blood yet is no troll? Is it a riddle?"

"I am an elf troll," Little Fur told her, wondering what a riddle was.

The kid considered this for a moment, then trotted away with an incredulous snort.

Little Fur went to the nearest pear tree and laid her palm against its bark. Like all trees seeded in the age of humans, it was not completely awake, but she had once taken the seeds of this tree to plant in the grove of the Old Ones, and she wanted to give it news of them. The pear tree stirred and Little Fur was startled to be offered a fleeting picture of herself planting the seedlings. The Old Ones must have sent the vision into the flow of earth magic. Little Fur shivered at the thought of the Old Ones communing with the earth spirit about her.

The pear tree drifted back into its dream. Little Fur went on her way, sniffing contentedly at the heavy brown perfume rising from the thick mulch of fallen leaves that lay below the trees.

Beyond the pear orchard was another field. Little Fur made her way carefully across it to where Ginger patiently waited. She had to avoid the flabby numbness of the dead patches of soil. At the edge of the field, she knelt beside a dead patch and took a little bit of moist moss and a seed from her pouch. She pressed the seed into the moss, then pushed both into the ground, making sure a little of the moss touched the good earth as well as the dead earth. Then she sang a song to encourage the seed to life.

I am like a mouse nibbling at the edge of a mountain, Little Fur thought as she stood up. But she was smiling as she closed her seed pouch. Being small, she had no contempt for small triumphs. If a mouse lived long enough, it might nibble away a mountain of cheese, and she was an elf troll, with the blood of two long-lived races mingling in her. There was no telling how many seeds she could plant before she entered the world's dream.

"Craaak! Hurrying," Crow cawed, swooping low so that his feathers brushed the tips of her furled ears. She laughed up at him and quickened her pace, dropping her hand to Ginger's soft coat.

Soon they came to the high, square-trimmed hedge beyond which lay the beaked house. Crow had flown over it, but suddenly he veered sharply back and landed on the grass beside Little Fur.

"Are humans there?" she asked. She knew two humans tended the beaked house, but they usually left when the sun closed its eye.

"Craaak! Not humans. Owls," Crow cawed urgently. "A manyness of owls. Crow must going.

48

Maybe they gathering to hunting all crows." He flapped into the air and away.

Little Fur looked at Ginger. "Maybe the Sett Owl foresaw my question and has summoned the owls in readiness." She crawled on hands and knees under another fence and beneath the tough black branches of the hedge, eager for the strange, thrilling sight of the beaked house. Rising on the other side of the hedge, she saw that the crossed sticks fastened to the steeply pointed roof of the beaked house were dark against the brightness of a full moon.

Little Fur glanced about uneasily, even though humans usually came in the daytime, when the custodians opened the doors. They came, Crow had claimed, to sing. Little Fur had laughed at the idea of humans singing, until she had smelled the power that rose from their songs like smoke from fire. It was now her belief that human singing had some connection to the powerful pool of magic within the beaked house.

Little Fur slipped through a barrier of metal spikes. She had no need to worry about where she set her feet, because the yard she entered was cobbled in flat, moss-velveted stones. Earth magic ran freely and strongly about them, though it ended abruptly at the beaked house. Within its walls, the still magic had dominion.

An owl hooted. Little Fur saw that owls were perched along the roof in every niche and on every piece of jutting stonework. She made her way to the other side of the beaked house, passing the front steps that led to the massive doors. The doors were firmly shut, and she continued until she could see the enormous tree that grew on the other side of the building. Planted on the cusp of the human age, the tree was not quite asleep nor yet awake, but it knew Little Fur.

She came closer to greet it. But when her feet pressed down on the great crackling carpet of fallen leaves that lay about its humped roots, she looked up and saw that what she had taken for its foliage was in fact hundreds of owls. Still won-

dering if the Sett Owl had foreseen her visit,
Little Fur went to the opening at the base of
the wall that led under it and into the beaked

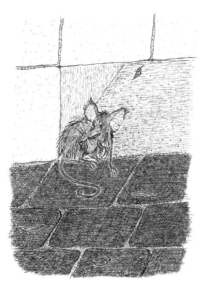

house's immense chamber. To her surprise, a great crowd of animals and birds was gathered at the opening. Barring their way was the Sett Owl's attendant, a sleek rat named Gazrak. He was bristling with fury, and Little Fur could smell that some sort of argument was in progress. She moved closer, turning her soft ears, the better to hear.

CHAPTER 5
A Convocation of Owls

"You will have to come back later," Gazrak told the assembled animals in a peevish voice that suggested he had said the same thing more than once already. "Herness is very busy," he added pompously. "Very, *very* busy."

"We have crossed half the city to speak to the Sett Owl," said a drake. A small cluster of ducks about him quacked indignantly in agreement. "We came at great risk!" the drake added firmly.

"We *all* come here at risk," chittered a red squirrel.

The rat turned his long twitching nose and slitted red eyes to the squirrel and hissed. "Gazrak can't help that. You can't see Herness until the owl convocation is over."

"Well, how long is this convocation going to take?" asked a white cat in a pretty, purring voice. A goose hissed softly to warn her not to get too close, but the cat gave him an amused look. "Keep your feathers on, father," she told him coolly, and turned her attention back to the rat.

"The owl convocation will take as long as it takes," Gazrak said haughtily.

"What are we supposed to do, then?" demanded a weasel. The rat glared at her, then turned his eyes shiftily to the offerings that rose in a tantalizing little mound in front of the drake.

"You will have to come back. But you can leave your offerings. I will make sure that the Sett Owl gets them and knows who is owed an audience."

"Not on your life," snapped a stoat. "I'd sooner trust a snake than a rat to keep a promise."

"Watch who you are insssulting," hissed a snake, uncoiling to glare at the stoat.

"No fighting! It is forbidden for supplicants to fight in the grounds of the beaked house. Fighting is sacreligion," shrilled the rat.

"What I would like to know is when this convocation began," asked a deep, slow voice from somewhere in the crowd. It sounded like a sensible sort of voice, and Little Fur guessed it was a badger's.

The rat eyed the gathering balefully. "Herness sent out the pigeons at dusk yesterday, and owls began arriving soon after. The Sett Owl has been interviewing them all night, and there are many owls still waiting to see her."

There was a disgruntled murmur. Some of the animals glumly gathered up their offerings and departed. Gazrak went back into the tunnel in a fury, leaving those who remained to argue over what to do.

Little Fur returned to where Ginger sat watching stray feathers drifting down from the tree of owls. "The Sett Owl is questioning all of the owls, but no one knows why," Little Fur told him.

"Little Fur could also question owls," Ginger said.

Little Fur realized the cat was right. She had wanted to see the Sett Owl only so she could speak to other owls. The mother of the orphaned owl might even be here. Little Fur walked under the lowest branch of the tree, which creaked under the weight of a great horned owl, two ghostly-looking barn owls and several smaller owls. They blinked orange and yellow eyes at her.

"Greetings, Owls," Little Fur said very

politely, for owls have a keen sense of ceremony. "I am —"

"Whoo hoo, we know who you are, Little Fur," said the horned owl. "What do you want of us, Healer?"

Little Fur did not know whether to be gratified or unnerved that it knew who she was. She bowed and began, "I came to see the Sett Owl —"

"Whoo! She is busy with owl business," said a smaller owl. "She has called a convocation."

"Hush," said one of the other owls. "The great questioning is owl business."

"Too true," hooted the smaller owl.

"My business is also owl business," Little Fur assured them. There was a rustling of feathers all about her, but none of the owls spoke, so she went on. "What I wanted to find out was if any of you here has lost a nestling, or knows of an owl who lost a nest with young in it during the storm last night."

The horned owl said loftily, "The night was full

of falling nests and broken eggs." There was a rustle of agreement from the other owls.

"I am speaking of a particular nest and a particular nestling," Little Fur said. "Is there an owl mother among you who is grieving for her lost young?"

"Whoo hoo," said the horned owl, waggling its feathery horns at her. "Owls do not make the mistake of getting too attached to eggs or nestlings. They are not strongly enough attached to life. It would be—"

"Foolish," completed one of the barn owls.

Little Fur was puzzled. "I just meant—"

"Forgetting the loss of nestlings is natural and also more comfortable than pointless grieving over a broken egg," said an owl from one of the other branches.

"But what if an egg falls and does not break, or breaks only to free its nestling?" Little Fur asked.

The horned owl said, "The chance of life after the fall is minus. Very minus."

Little Fur was becoming exasperated. "I am

speaking of a particular nestling which fell but did *not* die," she said.

"We do not think of what happens after the fall," intoned the horned owl. Little Fur felt an urge to pull its tail feathers. Owls were cleverer than other birds, but they had their limitations. She walked around the tree asking other owls the same question. Over and over, she was given the same answer.

Finally, she came to an owl who had lost her nest in the storm. "Many eggs and nestlings are lost in the lifetime of a bird," she told Little Fur calmly. "It is not in the nature of owls, who see more deeply and wisely than other birds, to sit on hope and seek to hatch it into the lost nestling. As it falls from the nest, the egg or nestling falls from one's heart, lest grief take root and grow to crack the spirit apart."

"But this owlet . . ." Little Fur began. Then she stopped, not certain what she wanted to say.

". . . will live or die," the owl mother said.

And that seemed to be that.

Exhausted and baffled, Little Fur went back to sit on the step beside Ginger. "The owls say that once an egg or owlet falls out of the nest, the mother forgets it. They say that there is no point in their caring when so many eggs die. I will have to wait to see the Sett Owl after all. Perhaps she will order the owls who have lost nests to come to the wilderness. I am sure if they could see the baby owl and know she is their own, they would be glad to claim her."

Ginger held Little Fur's gaze until she saw what he did not say: the Sett Owl would not order any of the owls to do anything, because she did not give orders. She answered questions. *Well then,* Little Fur thought, *I will ask the Sett Owl how to get the baby owl back to its mother.*

Too restless to sleep or sit, Little Fur rose and began to walk around the beaked house again. She was curious about this convocation. One of the owls had named it a great questioning. Since the Sett Owl had called the owls together, she must be asking them questions. But what could an ordinary owl know that she did not?

Little Fur saw a fox sitting by the front steps of the beaked house. It was a big fox, but she could clearly see its bones curving under its dull red pelt. She sniffed and caught the hot bright stink of pain and the dank odor of infection. "Can I help you?" she asked, going over to it.

The fox turned its head to look at her. It was a male, she smelled now, handsome and well formed. Or he would have been, if not for his unkempt pelt and his thinness. His deep brown eyes were not clouded with pain, though, or with confusion. They were full

of intelligence, but their bleak expression chilled her.

"What do ye want?" the fox asked. There was an unfamiliar accent to his soft voice that told her he came from somewhere other than the city.

"I . . . I am a healer," Little Fur said. "I can smell that you are hurt and I thought I could help you."

"I do not wish to be helped," the fox said.

Little Fur was taken aback. "But . . . you would not be here unless you wanted help. . . ."

"Are ye so wise as to know my thoughts and intentions better than I do?" the fox asked coldly. "Perhaps I would do better to consult ye than the Sett Owl. However, I did not come here for healing, but to learn how to die."

Little Fur thought she must have misunderstood. "You are afraid you are going to die?"

"I want to die," the fox told her in a clear, stony voice, "but my will to live is too strong. I heard of the wisdom of the Sett Owl and I have come very far to see if she can tell me how to die. And now that ye have satisfied your curiosity, ye can leave me alone."

Little Fur had never before had her healing refused. She went to Ginger, who was sleeping, and laid her cheek against him, seeking the reassuring beat of his heart. The encounter with the fox had unsettled her. He had said that he wished to die but could not. His instinct to live must be very powerful, she thought, for creatures did die by willing it. She had seen it in old animals who had grown weary of life and struggle and pain, in the remaining member of a life-bonded pair and sometimes in a mother who had lost a child. But the fox was neither mother nor elder, and he had such an absolute air of solitude that she did not think he had lost a mate.

She drifted to sleep and it seemed but a moment before Ginger was turning to lick her cheek with his warm, rough tongue.

"It has finished," he said.

CHAPTER 6
The Sett Owl Speaks

Little Fur sat up. The sky was the pure, starless blue of very early morning, and owls were flying away in all directions. For a moment or two, it was as if there were a snowstorm in the air. Hundreds of pale, soft feathers drifted down to whiten the cobbles beneath the bare, reaching black arms of the tree.

"You," the rat said decisively, pointing his black paw at Little Fur and ignoring the irritable yowl of a white cat and the grumblings of a weasel. "And you." He pointed to the fox.

Then he selected a vole and a mouse on the fringe, both recent arrivals. Little Fur was so relieved to be able to go in at once that she didn't argue for fairness. She crawled into the tunnel after Ginger, who had announced to Gazrak that he needed no permission to enter since he sought no answer for himself.

The huge chamber that was the interior of the beaked house smelled of polished wood, shining metals, and a strange spice that mingled with the scent of dying roses, which humans had brought as offerings. The smooth, dark flagstones gave off a reflection of the red glow of human false lights fixed to the walls of the chamber.

Little Fur did not climb out of the tunnel as the others had done, because there was no flow of earth magic within the beaked house. The mouse and vole gazed about in awe and apprehension. The fox sniffed the end of one of the wooden benches where humans sometimes sat, a flicker of loathing crossing his features, then looked at Little Fur as if he felt her watching. She quickly turned her eyes away and found herself staring at the feet of one of the enormous stone humans that stood all about the chamber, each in its own niche in the wall.

Gazrak came along the tunnel behind Little Fur and grumbled loudly when he found her blocking the way. Pushing past her, he hurried over to where the vole and mouse had laid down their offerings—a few nuts, late berries and crusts. Little Fur dug a packet of herbs from her seed pouch and reached out as far as she could to put it beside the other things. The still magic quivered against her cheeks as Gazrak inspected the offering suspiciously.

"What is this?" he demanded.

"Herbs to ease the pain of the Sett Owl's crippled wing," Little Fur said with shy dignity.

"Pah," the rat jeered, but he passed on to the fox. "Where is your offering?"

"I did not know that I needed one," the fox said. He was sitting with his tail curved around him. His air of solitary completeness struck Little Fur anew.

"Herness is not interested in excuses," Gazrak snarled. "You must leave! Come back when you have a properness of offering for Herness."

"Wait," Little Fur said. "I have some fresh mushrooms that I brought for my supper. If those would do . . . ?" She set them alongside the packet of herbs. The rat crept closer, his nose twitching.

"I cannot allow ye to pay for me," the fox said. "That would mean I would owe ye a debt, and I do not wish to owe anything to any creature."

"You don't have to pay me," Little Fur said. "The mushrooms can be a gift."

"Then ye offer a friendship that I did not seek and do not desire. Take them back." He turned to the rat. "I will go, and return when—"

"Enough of this foolishness." The voice of the Sett Owl rang out from above. "Do not be so quick to spurn friendship, Master Fox."

They all looked up to see her spiraling down from the shadows clustered beneath the roof. Her damaged wing made the descent uneven. She landed with a staggering awkwardness that filled

Little Fur's nostrils with the scent of pain and stiffness.

"He has brought no offering," Gazrak whined to his mistress, who had landed on one of the wooden benches. "What are we to eat if—"

"Silence, Rat," the Sett Owl commanded. "*I* might starve without offerings, but you are fat enough to last for a full cycle of the moon. Now be silent unless you wish to offer yourself as a meal out of reverence to me."

The rat gave a shriek of terror and scuttled away.

The owl turned to the fox, who bowed his head in a handsome gesture and said politely but sternly, "I would not be indebted to ye either, Herness."

"Whoo! You! Oh, you will pay for your questions, Master Fox. Have no fear." The owl's voice was chalky with humor. She turned her flaring eyes to Little Fur, still crouched at the opening of the tunnel. "It is good to see you again, Healer. I am grateful for your offering, and you may keep your supper if you will brew the tisane for me. But come out where I can see you properly."

"I can't," Little Fur said. "I would be cut off from the flow of the earth magic if I came into the beaked house."

The Sett Owl regarded her without expression. Then she said, "Put one foot out onto the floor."

Little Fur hesitated, then obeyed, lowering her four toes gingerly to the floor. She knew that no harm would come to her as long as some part of her stayed on the earth floor of the tunnel. To her amazement, she felt earth magic surging against her foot.

"I don't understand," she whispered.

"I have asked the still magic to allow the passage of earth magic. Now enter," the owl said. "How else will you prepare my tisane?"

Heart beating fast, Little Fur put both feet out onto the flagstones, keeping her bottom firmly on the earth floor of the tunnel. Earth magic flowed to the soles of her feet. Very slowly, she stood up and looked around. Above the tunnel was the statue of a winged woman holding out a slender white hand. The bubbling sensation that was the still magic pressed and nuzzled at Little Fur like

some invisible and inquisitive animal wanting to smell her better.

"Have no fear that the earth magic will fail under you," the owl said mildly. "Still magic and earth magic are not inimical to one another. It is only that both are very strong and are content to be apart." The owl turned to greet Ginger courteously; then she spoke to the smaller creatures who had drawn together. She accepted their offerings and dealt quickly but kindly with their timid questions. Finally, only the fox, Little Fur and Ginger remained.

"Well now, Healer," the Sett Owl said. "The storm orphan."

Little Fur nodded, unsurprised to find that the Sett Owl knew why she had come. If the still magic had not told her, the owls she had spoken to would have done so.

"You are not content with the answers you have been given by my brethren?" the Sett Owl inquired.

"I understand what they are saying, but I don't

understand why the owls who have lost nestlings won't just come and see if the baby is theirs."

"For an owl, to fall *is* to die."

Little Fur felt a surge of frustration. "I do not think the owlet who fell and lived would agree."

"You and the fox come on the same errand, then," observed the Sett Owl. "You both seek to thwart nature. That is a very human desire."

Little Fur was shocked to be likened to humans. But the snarl of the fox overshadowed her reaction. "I have no human desires," he said in a voice so raw with hatred that Little Fur thought he would leap at the owl and tear her to pieces.

The Sett Owl gazed at him without fear. "The human way is to set will against nature."

"I do not wish to speak of humans or of nature," the fox said in a low, angry voice.

"Nor do I," the owl said with sudden weariness. "I have spoken too much of these things already this long night. Well, ask your question, Fox."

"Ye know it already," the fox said. "I wish to die, but my instinct to live chains me to life. I want to know how I can overcome my instinct."

"You wish to join the world's dream?" the owl asked.

"It is not known what comes after life, and I think none *can* know, for none who die return to say what they have seen. For myself, I hope there is no dream."

"Some say the world's dream is no more than a long remembering of all that was and all that will be," the owl murmured.

"I did not come to talk about memories either, Herness," the fox said shortly.

"Very well. An answer to your question. You cannot overcome your instinct to live, because its great strength is of your own long making."

"Then ye cannot help me."

"I cannot help you defeat your will to survive, for you have trained it to be indomitable. But perhaps I can suggest a way for you to find death."

The fox's eyes narrowed. "How?"

"You must seek a road to death that does not oppose your will to survive."

"Ye speak in riddles," the fox said.

Little Fur's ears prickled to hear the strange word again.

"Life is a riddle, Fox," the Sett Owl told him. "One cannot speak simply of such a mystery. Now listen to me. If you wish to die, then you must give yourself wholly to a deadly quest. You must make it more important than your life. Only then will your instinct permit the sacrificing of life, should it be required by the quest."

The fox regarded the Sett Owl steadily for a long moment. "Ye have such a quest in mind?"

"I do," the owl said composedly. "A plot against the earth spirit is being hatched in this city, or to be precise, *beneath* the city, in the troll stronghold of Underth. You have heard of it?"

"I have heard of the troll city, but I understood it to be a myth. What would ye have me do? Set out to kill its king, if he exists?"

"He exists," the owl said softly.

"What, then?" the fox asked.

"All night I have sought information in an attempt to guess what the Troll King plots. I have found no answer but this: an expedition must be mounted to Underth to discover the Troll King's plans."

"The storm," the fox said thoughtfully. "There were omens in it. . . ."

"We must learn the nature of the danger. Without that knowledge, we cannot hope to defend the earth spirit. The omens say that if it is not defended, the Troll King will bring an age of darkness to the earth that will see the end of many things."

"If I undertake to travel to Underth to get this knowledge, and if the stories of it and of the trolls that guard it are even partly true, my death is almost certain. That will serve *my* desire, but how will it serve yours? How will ye discover what I have learned?" the fox asked.

"You will have companions," the owl said.

"I travel alone," the fox replied at once.

"You will need a guide to lead you from the surface to the troll city. It is not just a matter of finding a way through myriad tunnels and holes. There are also the dark confusions of magic brewed by the Troll King, which affect any creature not born under his dominion."

The fox broke in. "Ye spoke of *companions*."

"Indeed. You are too big and brightly colored to gather the information that is needed. That will require spies who can swim in the shadows and slip through small cracks and crannies."

"If my companions are to be guides and spies, then why am I needed?" asked the fox. "I do not understand."

"You will be the warrior who guards the expedition. You will protect your fellow expeditioners, even at the cost of your own life. You must be prepared to offer yourself as a decoy and draw danger away from your companions, that they may bring what has been learned to me."

"Even if I agree, the chance of anyone escaping will be slim," the fox said.

"In asking you to swear to place their safety above your own, I bestow upon them the protection of your ferocious will to survive. They can have no greater shield."

There was a long silence. "Who will be the spies and the guide?" the fox asked.

Little Fur had the dreamy certainty that the Sett Owl would name her, but the owl merely said, "Two ferrets have volunteered as spies."

"And the guide?"

"The rat Gazrak, who is my attendant. He knows the way to Underth, and having been born there, he will be immune to the glamours set up to trap intruders," the Sett Owl said.

Out of the shadows at the back of the beaked house came a squeal of anguish and dismay.

CHAPTER 7

A Quest into Darkness

"No! Gazrak will not go! No! Noooo!" the rat snarled.

The Sett Owl merely watched until he had cringed and whimpered and hissed himself to silence. "You will go," she said.

Cunning flickered in the rat's eyes. "But, Herness, who will care for you when I am gone?" he said in a wheedling voice.

"That is not your concern, Gazrak. You will guide the fox and his companions to Underth, and when you return, you will be welcome."

The rat whined and trembled and shook his head some more. Little Fur thought Gazrak was rude and greedy, but it still did not seem right to force him to undertake such a dangerous quest against his will. The owl seemed to hear her thought.

"The rat has a debt that blackens his spirit. I gave Gazrak refuge here when the still magic would have rejected him, on the understanding that a day would come when I would require a duty which he must perform."

"But not this! Not there! They will kill me. They will eat me!" the rat shrilled.

"The fox will protect you," said the Sett Owl.

The fox replied, in a tone full of lifeless mockery, "It would be a fitting end to my life to die defending such a one."

"No! No!" The rat dived into the tunnel and vanished.

"The rat seems unwilling," the fox said.

"Gazrak will do as I have bidden," the Sett Owl replied with a touch of sadness.

"And the ferrets?"

"They are volunteers. I do not yet see your other companions, nor can I see when they will join you," the owl answered tranquilly.

"Wonderful," the fox murmured dryly. "An unknown army which will assemble at some unknown moment, no doubt. Is there anything else ye can foresee? The success of the expedition, perhaps?"

"I have seen that there is hope if it is mounted, and none if it is not. But there is another thing that I have foreseen which may be useful for you to know: one of those who accompany you will betray you."

"What?!" the fox exclaimed, for the first time looking incredulous. "Ye would have me go on so vital an expedition with a betrayer?"

"Without them all, the quest will fail."

The fox gave a dour bark of laughter. "Your

offer is compelling, Herness. To undertake an expedition that is almost certainly impossible, with unknown companions, one of whom will betray the rest. I accept. When do we leave? When the moon is blacked, or in the dead of winter, when snow freezes the earth? Or perhaps in the eye of the sun under the noses of the humans that infest the city?"

"You must leave when day comes," the owl responded. "The Troll King, his chief captains and a good part of his army are mustering for a journey along a subterranean road to a city by the sea. If you leave when I have proposed, you will miss the Troll King and his army and find a city peopled by lower trolls with dull wits and slow minds, who, in the absence of their master, will discuss his plans and intentions. It is they who must be sought out and spied upon."

"How long will this meeting of trolls take?"

"It will take the Troll King one day to reach the city by the sea," the owl said. "The same amount of time as it will take you to reach the tunnels and caverns above Underth if you leave when the sun opens its eye this day. You will then have three full days and nights to learn what you can. Then you must come back to the surface, or run the risk of meeting the returning Troll King and his army."

The fox was thoughtful for a while. Then he said, "Did ye foresee me coming here tonight?"

"I saw you enter the city," the owl said.

"What would ye have done if I had not come here?"

Instead of answering him, the owl turned to Little Fur. "Healer, I have pondered your question and this is my answer. The way forward is not to go backward. The owlet, whom nature would have killed, was saved first by the cat and then by you. The falling and the saving set it on a path away from clan and kin. There is no going back. The orphan is now your responsibility. Unless you abandon her."

Little Fur sighed. "Of course we won't abandon her, but I don't see how an owl can grow up into a proper owl mothered by a cat and an elf troll."

"Who is to say what is a proper owl?" the Sett Owl asked distantly.

Little Fur knew that was all the answer she was going to get, but she still wanted to know more about the fox and his quest. "Shall I brew your tisane now, Herness?"

The Sett Owl inclined her head with a twinkle in her eyes. Little Fur did not dare to look at the fox. She set about preparing the tisane, losing her self-consciousness as she concentrated on adding the herbs carefully in the right order. When she was finished, she carried the little wooden bowl of tisane to where the owl perched on one of the human bench seats and set it down carefully. She was about to pack her things away when the owl suggested that Little Fur might tend the fox's wounds.

"I want no healing!" the fox said sharply.

Little Fur hesitated; then, emboldened by what the owl had said, she murmured, "If you do not let me treat your wounds, you ought to tell the Sett Owl that you won't go. I can smell infection deep enough to put you in a fever by tonight, and by tomorrow you will begin to lose the use of your leg."

The fox spoke at last. "Very well, but be quick."

Little Fur went through the contents of her pouch and laid out what she needed. Then she poured the remainder of the water from her bottle into another small bowl. She soaked a wad of soft cloth in it and began to bathe the numerous small wounds on the fox that were clogged with dirt and dried blood. None of the wounds were dangerously deep, and all but two of them, the most recent and the worst, had already been treated. She was puzzled, because the fox had so resisted her help.

As she worked, she noticed some strange things. The first was that all of the treated wounds were at different stages of healing. That meant they must have been inflicted at different times.

The second was that the wounds were oddly neat, as if a small creature with very sharp teeth had delicately bit into the fox again and again. Looking more closely, Little Fur found countless older scars all over the fox's body. Some were so old that the fox must have been a cub when they had been inflicted.

The fox's obvious hatred of humans made

Little Fur certain that they were responsible for his wounds. Perhaps a human had kept the fox as a pet for the dark pleasure of hurting it. Or maybe the fox had escaped from the mysterious place Crow had told her about, beyond the outer edge of the city. Zoo, he had named it, describing walled enclosures and cages where many different kinds of animals were held captive.

Little Fur wished she could just ask the fox, but he was rigidly silent under her hands. She sensed that his whole being was focused on forcing himself to sit still as she tended to him. She left the deep cuts along his flank till last. Already, invisible but poisonous threads of infection had spread out from them in a fine and dangerous web. She bathed them thoroughly, then pressed a pollen and honey mix into them. Lastly, she used a fine bone threaded with plied spider's silk to sew the flaps of skin back together. She left a tiny opening at the end, where the wounds could drain. Throughout all of her ministrations, the fox grunted only once.

Finally, Little Fur smoothed a salve over the sewn cuts, feeling delicately along the outline of the long leg bones as she did to be sure they were not fractured or chipped. Again she found something curious. The bones were not broken, but there were bumps all along them as if they had been broken in the distant past, not once but many times.

"That is enough," the fox said tightly, moving away from her touch.

She nodded. "You need to rest—"

"I will sleep after the expedition," he said.

Little Fur wanted to argue but she said only, "I will mix you a tisane to take with you. It will help the wounds to knit more quickly and it will numb the pain."

"Anything else?" the fox asked ironically.

"Yes," Little Fur said. "You must eat now, for what I have done has drained your strength." She turned to Gazrak, who had returned and was glaring at them. "Can you bring some food and some more water? And do you have a bottle with a stopper?"

"Bottle! Food! Water!" The rat's eyes blazed with outrage, but he scuttled away. By the time Little Fur's things had been cleaned and returned to their places in the pouch, the rat had come back with a bulging cloth full of food and a small bottle like her own, made from a gourd and filled with water. He flung them down with a hiss and darted away.

"The rat will be a pleasant companion," the fox observed.

"You should eat," Little Fur urged.

"What is your name, Healer?" the fox asked.

Little Fur told him shyly.

"I am Sorrow," the fox said. "I asked your name and I tell ye my own, for I owe ye a debt."

"Why did your mother name you Sorrow?" Little Fur asked.

"I have no memory of mother nor father nor den kin. For a black age, I lived without any idea of what sort of creature I was, or any knowledge that there were others like me. When I learned the truth, I found my name," the fox answered.

Little Fur did not know what to say to this. She had no memory of *her* father or mother either, and sometimes it saddened her that she could not remember them. But she could not deeply mourn what she had not known, or blame her parents or the world for their mysterious absence. But maybe it was not the lack of family that caused the fox his sorrow, but the circumstances in which he had learned that he was an orphan, especially if they were connected to the long history of scarring on his body. Little Fur wanted to ask about it, but the fox's grief was like one of the shining human high houses, which could be seen from anywhere in the city but could never be entered.

The fox would not eat, and finally he went outside, saying he could not sleep inside the beaked house because the stink of humans was too strong. Little Fur waited until he had gone, then asked the owl if she would like some more of the tisane.

"As payment for the question you now wish to ask me?" the Sett Owl asked shrewdly.

Little Fur hung her head. "I did want to ask you something."

"You are curious about the fox," the owl said.

"Is it wrong?" she asked humbly.

The Sett Owl's answer was kind. "There is no evil in your curiosity. It arises from your healing senses, Little Fur, and you need not feel shamed by it. But the questions you ask must be put to the fox himself. Yet know this one thing: for him, sorrow is a remembering and a reverence."

"I have touched the fox," Little Fur said slowly. "The scars on his body are nothing compared to the scarring of his spirit. Though I have healed his wounds, his ailing spirit will eventually undo all I have done. Quite soon, he will have his wish, whether or not he goes on this expedition."

"We have no hope but the strength of his will," the Sett Owl said.

"It does not seem . . . honest to use the sickness of a creature to solve a problem," Little Fur said.

"A great darkness looms over the world, and if it comes, this one fox's sickness will be as a single drop in a deluge of pain."

"You are saying that the earth spirit is more important than the fox?"

"Yes," the owl said.

Little Fur was silent for a time, mixing the tisane. "When I was healing his wounds, I was as careful and gentle as I could be, yet the fox shrank from my touch. Is it because I am part troll?"

"The fox shrank from his memories."

Little Fur sighed. This mystery was too bleak and deep for her. She looked at the owl again, into those enormous eyes. "Do you know where he is now?"

"The fox sleeps under the hedge where your crow companion skulks, clacking his beak. The fox's dreams are full of blood and pain, but they will not last long, for already a red dawn stains the sky."

CHAPTER 8
The Black Dog

"Where are the spies?" The fox seemed refreshed by his brief rest.

"The ferrets are waiting outside," the Sett Owl said. "Kell and Shikra are their names. They are brother and sister. Gazrak you have met."

Hearing his name, the rat emerged from a tangle of shadows, red eyes full of malice and terror.

"Ye said there would be others. I don't suppose ye have managed to see any of their faces as I slept?" the fox asked.

Little Fur felt the still magic in the beaked house swirling wildly and she heard herself answering, as if in a dream. "I will go."

The fox turned to stare at her. "I want no healer," he said coldly.

"What you want does not matter," the owl said. "Your chance of success is greater with the healer by your side. While you slept, I saw that your company will number nine." She glanced up at the long, narrow windows above the raised part of the floor, where faint light was beginning to strain through the jewel-like colors. "It is time for you to leave."

Sorrow still stared accusingly at Little Fur. "Underth is no place for a healer. If ye fall into their hands ye may wish to be dead. Have ye thought of that?"

"If the earth spirit is hurt by whatever it is that the Troll King is planning," Little Fur said softly, "all the world will be wounded and it will be a wound that no healer can mend, however skilled."

"So be it, then," said the fox.

And so they gathered: Little Fur; the fox called Sorrow; Gazrak, reeking of resentment and fear; and the brother and sister ferrets, *Brave* Kell (as he called himself) and Shikra. The ferrets wore small backpacks containing water bottles. Little

Fur carried her own pouches, into which she had put a small package of dried leaves, given to her by the Sett Owl, which would hide the true scent of anyone who rubbed it on their skin or fur.

Little Fur dropped her hand to Ginger's soft pelt after they slipped through the encircling spiked fence. She hoped the cat did not mean to accompany her farther than the troll hole that would lead them to Underth. She had drawn him into danger before, and she did not want to do it again.

They had gone only a few steps when Crow swooped to the ground. Gazrak screamed, but Crow ignored him.

"This being a great stupidness, Little Fur," he cawed, glaring at her. "You not having weapon to fighting trolls. Must not going on this expedition!"

"The Sett Owl—" Little Fur began.

"Sett Owl full of trickiness!" Crow screeched.

Little Fur looked at Ginger, but the gray cat made no comment.

Crow gave a sharp croak of frustration. "Must

 coming back to wilderness. That where you belonging. What Old Ones saying about this, eh?"

Little Fur said softly, "The Old Ones know what I do and why."

"Enough talking with this crow. We must go at once!" hissed Gazrak, who had recovered from his fright. He turned his red eyes up to the sky, which was growing brighter by the second.

"Yes," Little Fur said. "I'm sorry, Crow. I wish you could understand."

He took to the sky, and as they continued, she could feel him circling high overhead.

"He does not wish to lose you," Ginger said quietly.

"The Sett Owl said there is no hope for the

earth spirit if we do not find out what the Troll King is planning. She did not ask me to go, or even suggest it. But when I offered, she said there is a better chance of success if I do." Little Fur was talking to the fox as much as to Ginger. Sorrow had said nothing throughout Crow's tirade, but she had smelled his approval of the bird's opposition. Of course, she could not tell Sorrow that *her* purpose in going was not to fight but to keep him alive. . . .

Gazrak brought them to an older part of the city where many of the stone houses were empty and half had tumbled down. Little Fur had not been here before. Everywhere she looked, there were boards fixed over doors or webs of wire. All of the front gardens she could see were tangled and unkempt, and the windows were like empty sockets. But Little Fur's heart thrilled, for earth magic ran freely about the ground, where grass and moss and small plants were growing in a wild, happy tangle amidst the ruins.

The sun had lifted its eye high enough now that light was pressing down into the night shadows still lying damp and heavy in the cobbled lane. It would not be long before the shadows were vanquished. Then they would have to be very careful, for although this area was abandoned, it belonged to humans.

Little Fur thought of the owlet that she had left in the tree hollow. The Sett Owl had all but said that she must become its family, and yet here she was, setting off on a dangerous journey from which she might not return. Now she saw the wisdom behind the cruel-seeming philosophy of the owls about nests and fallen eggs, because life was full of unexpected abandonments. Perhaps her own parents had left her meaning to return, but had been unable to do so.

She looked up. There was no sign of Crow, but the bond between them told her that he was near. The thought of going away from him was heavy in her heart.

They came to a lane that crossed over the one

they were following. Sunlight flared on the walls of some of the buildings. Gazrak stopped abruptly and hissed at the brightness. The rest of them waited as he sniffed and twitched and chewed at the ends of his paws before springing forward. As they hastened after him, Little Fur thought what an uncomfortable journey it would be if it must be made with such sudden stops and bursts of manic speed. There was no doubt in her mind that Gazrak knew exactly where he was going, though.

"It is getting very lightful," said Shikra to her brother.

"Soon we will go into darkness," he answered.

The ferrets' fur was deep gold at the throat, matching the gold flecks in their brown eyes, but their bodies were a deeper shade, brown misted with gray and black. In the shadows, they were almost invisible, even to Little Fur's eyes. The owl was right about their being the perfect spies. Beside them, the fox's fur and brush were like a tongue of fire, and she knew her own hair was no less vivid.

At length, inevitably, a black road ran across their path. Little Fur explained that she must find some way to cross it that would not sever her from the flow of earth magic.

"We cannot wait!" the rat snarled, glaring frantically at the sun. "You must find your own way across and follow us."

The fox looked at Ginger. "Ye will stay with her?"

"Always," said Ginger very quietly.

Little Fur watched the rat, the two ferrets and the fox cross the black road and make their way down the cobbled lane on the other side. They had gone out of sight when Crow spiraled out of nowhere to land beside her.

"Now is timeliness for going back to wilderness," he said.

"Crow, I can't," Little Fur said firmly. "But will you help me to cross the black road?"

He gave a disgruntled croak and took to his

wings. Her eyes followed as he flew high and then banked left, out of sight, behind a building. Soon he flew back to report that the road was narrower and more broken in that direction.

Little Fur set off at once. Crow came hippity-hopping along beside her and reminded her of all the stories of savage trolls they had heard.

Little Fur needed no reminding. "Dear Crow," she said, "when I had to leave the wilderness the first time, there were terrible risks, but you understood why I had to go. It is the same now."

"But Crow cannot coming with you under the ground!" Crow cawed forlornly. "Who will watching for danger?"

"My eyes see well in the darkness. My claws are sharp," Ginger said with a soft fierceness that made his orange eyes flash. Little Fur's heart clenched. Partly she was glad that the cat was determined to come with her, but what if something happened to him on the way to Underth?

"Trolls seeing better. Their claws being sharper," Crow muttered.

"I made a promise."

"Promise!" Crow cried. "Who caring of promisings? Trolls will eating you! They will sucking the marrow out of your bones! Then what will your promisings be but meat in troll's hairy belly?"

"I have said I will go," Little Fur insisted. "Maybe the troll bit of me will help." She touched the green rock at her throat that was a gift from her troll mother, as her lost cloak had been a gift from her elf father. Of course, she did not remember the giving of either, but what else could those two things be but gifts?

They came to an older part of the road. Grass grew up thickly through the cracks. Unfortunately, there was no space to walk back along the road on the other side. Little Fur crossed anyway, Ginger by her side. Her previous expeditions into the city had shown her that eventually all of the roads in the city connected. In any case, it was growing late and each moment that passed

increased the danger of their being spotted by a human.

On the other side, Sorrow appeared, coming along the lane toward them.

"There is a dog in the lane where the troll hole is," he said at once. "The rat and the ferrets managed to get into the troll hole before the dog got to them. I sprang away to lead it aside, but it would not follow. It waits by the opening."

"Waits for what?" Little Fur asked. The idea of a dog terrified her.

"I do not know," the fox said impatiently. "I came to warn ye to turn back."

Little Fur frowned at him. "Are you giving up, then?"

"No. I do not fear the dog. I will fight it if I must and then join the others.

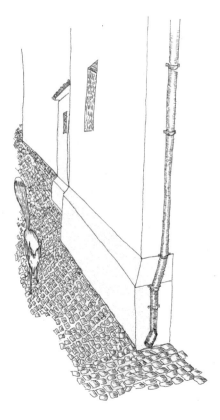

I swore an oath to the Sett Owl. But ye must go back to your wilderness."

"No," Little Fur said. "I made a promise, too, and it is no less important to me than your promise is to you."

The fox stared at her, pale shafts of gold and scarlet showing in his eyes. Without a word, he turned and padded back down the lane. Little Fur followed on legs that suddenly felt weak. As they approached a bend in the lane, she smelled the fury of the dog ahead. She clenched her teeth to stop them from rattling. The fox stepped around the corner into the sunlight, his pelt blazing. Little Fur tottered out into the light behind him.

Then Little Fur saw the enormous black dog barring their way. Her breath caught in her throat, for she knew this dog.

CHAPTER 9
A Painful Parting

"Move and let us pass, Dog," commanded Sorrow. He shone like a long lick of flame, the utter opposite of the midnight-black dog facing him.

"I have no quarrel with you, Fox," the dog announced in a husky voice that smelled to Little Fur of burnt flesh and singed fur.

"Then stand aside, She-dog," the fox said.

"I will not. But you and the cat may pass without harm. My business is with the thing from the last age that stands behind you."

The fox gave off the scent of disbelief mingled with genuine surprise. "The healer?"

"I swore to drink her blood and crunch her bones. She and the one-eyed cat," the dog snarled.

"I have never done harm to you," Little Fur managed, her voice as frail as a dry leaf.

"I swore," the dog repeated. "I escaped and followed the cat reek here. It is convenient that you are here, too. I will kill you, and then I will find the one-eyed cat and kill her."

"What is all of this?" Sorrow demanded.

"A cat called Sly tormented this dog when it was trapped. She taunted it and made it hurt itself. I don't know why," said Little Fur.

The fox sighed. "This night is full of conflicting oaths." He turned back to the dog. "Ye must kill me if ye would kill the healer, for I am on a quest and she is part of it."

"A quest! I care not," growled the dog, the smell of madness boiling out of her. "I will tear out the heart of your healer and then I will seek the other. The cat. I have dreamed of revenge over and over. I have dreamed of the salt taste of her wicked blood."

"Then ye have dreamed of death, for I cannot allow ye to touch one of our company," the fox said.

The dog snarled and crouched. Her muscles bunched in readiness to attack.

"Be glad of your hatred, Dog," the fox said in a voice so strange and hollow that the dog paused, "for rage fills ye with life and hot purpose. Know that if ye kill these two, ye will become as cold and empty as an old bone in the wind."

These words seemed to rise up from the very heart of the fox's mysterious grief. Little Fur shivered. The dog did not move or make any answer. But the smell of rage remained. Crow gave a cawing cry high in the air. Instinctively, the fox looked up, and the spell was broken.

The dog gave an enraged roar and lunged

toward Little Fur. Her great jaws opened. Little Fur's bones seemed to dissolve as she looked into that red swallowing darkness.

Ginger sprang, twisting in the air to land on the dog's back. He bit savagely, sinking his sharp claws deep so that he would not be thrown off. The dog bellowed in rage and pain, and whipped her head around to catch the gray cat in her teeth, but she could not reach him.

Now the fox leaped, too, mouth opening to reveal teeth like needles. He caught the dog on the ear and dragged her sideways. Ginger jumped away as the dog went down, and then he attacked again, clawing the dog's tender underbelly.

Little Fur could not bear it. "Oh, please!" she cried. "Stop! Don't kill the dog! Don't hurt her anymore!"

Her voice was shockingly loud. The harsh grunting and rasping sounds stopped.

Then the dog erupted into action again. She shook Ginger and Sorrow off like two kittens.

Little Fur realized that the dog had never been in any danger of being killed. It was the others who would die—and herself!

But instead of attacking, the dog approached Little Fur, the smell of madness and hatred fading into a muddle. Both Sorrow and Ginger were poised to spring again, but the change in her scent made them hesitate.

"You . . . told them to stop," the dog growled, her small eyes glaring down at Little Fur. "Why?"

"I . . . I thought they would kill you," she whispered.

"I would have killed *you* if they had not attacked. Why did you not urge them on?"

Little Fur felt sick from the hot, meaty reek of the dog. "I . . . I am a healer," she said.

The dog regarded her for a long moment, its scents shifting and changing. Suddenly Crow was swooping overhead and shrieking, "Craaak! *Humans coming!*"

Instantly the dog turned and bounded away

and out of sight. Sorrow leaped sideways through a small crumbled opening in the wall beside them. Little Fur and Ginger followed.

They found themselves in the remnants of a human garden. The fox went to ground behind some ripe, fat pumpkins in a tangle of weeds and

Ginger wove cat shadows about himself. Little Fur pressed herself against the wall and held her breath.

Over the drumming of her heart, Little Fur heard human voices and boots thudding on the cobbles. As the humans came nearer, she smelled anger and a black excitement. A few humans paused beside the opening in the wall. To her amazement, Little Fur could smell the black dog in their words. They were looking for her.

Now there was the roar of a road beast. It came into the lane with a long, horrible wailing cry that went on and on. Little Fur clapped her hands over her ears. Even through tightly closed eyes she could see great flashes of blue light like sky-fire. There were more humans and more talk, but all she could do was curl into a ball. At long last, the humans and the road beast went away. Little Fur did not dare to take her hands from her ears until Ginger nuzzled at her.

Sitting up shakily, she still seemed to hear the dreadful scream of the road beast, though all was quiet. She noticed the fox watching her. She expected him to tell her again that she ought to go back to the wilderness, but he only rose and slipped through the opening back into the cobbled lane. Little Fur stood up and climbed unsteadily after him.

There was no sign of Sorrow, but Ginger padded down the lane to the troll hole, where the black dog had been. The bitter smell of troll made Little Fur hesitate. Crow spiraled down to land on the cobbles.

"More humans come," he warned. "Little Fur not going down to Underth!"

"Crow, dear Crow, I must." Little Fur reached out to stroke his black plumage, shining in the sunlight. "Go back to the wilderness. Tell Tillet what has happened and help her to watch over the baby owl."

Before Crow could beg her again, Little Fur climbed into the troll hole. It led to a human cellar with an earth floor. The animals' eyes glimmered in the shadows.

"You are wasting time!" the rat accused.

"Then let us waste no more," Sorrow said coolly. He turned, and Little Fur saw that behind him the cellar floor opened to re-veal a wide crack with a ramplike path down into the earth. Sorrow leaped lightly into it and disappeared. Gazrak and the ferrets followed, leaving Little Fur and Ginger to bring up the rear. It grew darker as they descended, but Little Fur's troll blood helped her to see clearly. The animals did not need much light to see, and where there was no light, their noses guided them.

Little Fur felt the softness of Ginger's fur against her bare leg and was glad, though she was certain that the bond between them was responsible for his devotion, which made her feel that he did not really have any choice. The same bond told her that poor Crow was flying in frantic circles in the air above the troll hole. There was a physical pain in the separation.

Ginger pressed against her side and said softly, "Earth magic does not work against nature. It can only strengthen what already exists." Then he went ahead of her, and Little Fur stared after him. It was the first time any of them had spoken of their bond, and she had always wondered if she had imagined it.

The path leveled off, so it was easier to walk. Little Fur's nose told her that the crack was natural but had been widened by a burrowing animal before being used by trolls. Her troll blood also helped her feel that there were spikes and strands of human-made stuff pushed into the earth all around them. Some of these protruded into the tunnel they were passing along. She reached again to touch the green stone around her neck.

Little Fur was not tired when the fox called a halt, but when she sat, her knees and the fronts of her legs ached from the steep angle. Earth magic flowed through the ground around her, but it lacked the liveliness of the magic that ran closer to the surface, where there were growing things.

"How long is this tunnel?" Sorrow asked Gazrak.

"We have gone only a small part of the way to Underth," Gazrak said. "We must go on now. If a troll comes, there is no place here to hide."

They continued down, and Little Fur noted

changes in the earth about them. The yellowish clay with hard white stone and a sweet, elusive scent was replaced by chalky earth streaked with black that glittered with its own fierce radiance. At last, they came to the end of the path. It opened into the side of an enormous human tunnel. Little Fur saw with amaze- ment that twin metal rails ran along the tunnel floor.

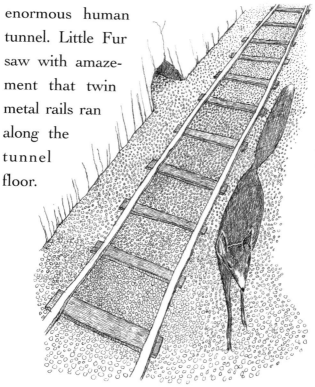

Aboveground she had seen such rails before, as well as the long metal snake with a single eye that had roared along them.

"Go quickly now," Gazrak said, "for the road serpents pass often and fill the tunnel with their roaring bulk."

"Go where?" Sorrow asked, sniffing the air.

"There is another troll hole farther along this human tunnel," Gazrak said. He scuttled off along the rails. Sorrow and the ferrets flowed after him, but Little Fur could not move so quickly. She did not want to touch the metal rails, for she could smell that they had been splashed with stinging poisons. Humans—she could smell them close by!

The tunnel curved and straightened. Little Fur saw light ahead; bright false light poured from a cave set high into the side of the tunnel. As they neared the cave, she could see humans moving about and looking along the tunnel. Little Fur realized they must be waiting for the road serpent. Perhaps this was another sort of beast feeding place.

The fox was making his way along the wall that ran beneath the opening to the cave. Little Fur pressed herself against the side of the tunnel and followed him. She had just gotten clear of the cave when wind began to tug at her hair. Puzzled, she turned to look back along the tunnel. Then the metal rails began to sing.

Terror clogged her throat as a road serpent roared into view, its glaring white eye blazing. But it was slowing; screeching and shuddering, it came to a halt beside the high cave. This *was* a feeding place!

Little Fur hurried on, praying the other troll hole was near. She stumbled again and again on the loose stones scattered over the rock floor of the tunnel, but she quickly righted herself. Ginger stopped each time until she had clambered to her feet.

Suddenly the road serpent screamed. The

tunnel had curved so that Little Fur could not see the metal serpent, but when the rails began to sing, she knew that they had only seconds to find the troll hole. Luckily, Little Fur saw Sorrow just a few steps ahead, at the mouth of an opening in the side of the tunnel. She and Ginger reached the hole as the road serpent came roaring into view. The fox and the ferrets made room for them as they squeezed in. The sound as the beast passed was deafening.

"Too slow!" Gazrak gnashed his yellow teeth at them all once the terrible creature had gone.

No one spoke as they set off on another downward path. Rougher but less steep than the last one, it brought them swiftly to a section that had been greatly altered by humans. They passed through many caverns strung with wires, and human-made tunnels lit by dazzling false lights. There were also holes made by humans that led straight to the surface, high over their heads. Sometimes Little Fur was startled, stepping into what she had thought was a pool of false light, only to find it was true sunlight. The smell of humans was strong, and Little Fur asked Gazrak if they were likely to encounter any.

"We would hear humans long before the great clumsy creatures would have a chance to see us," Gazrak sneered. "The real danger is trolls."

Little Fur said nothing, for she had seen that without Gazrak, they would have been utterly lost. There were so many passages and channels, all smelling of human and troll, yet the rat led them this way and that without hesitation, over wires, alongside pipes that gurgled with sluggish liquid and through tunnels. Little Fur had never imagined that humans had penetrated so deeply into the earth. It made her wonder what else they did that she could not imagine.

Only when they reached the level beneath the city where humans did not go did Gazrak allow a halt in a shallow cave. The two ferrets immediately shrugged off their packs and set out small portions of food. They paid no attention to Gazrak's demand that the guide ought to have twice the amount of food as his followers.

The smell of troll and human had stolen away Little Fur's hunger. Instead of eating, she drank water from her bottle while the others drank from minute wooden bowls the ferrets gave them. At her insistence, the rat passed her the gourd of herb mixture that Little Fur had made in the beaked house. As she cupped her hand for the fox to drink a mouthful of the tisane, a discreet sniff assured her that his wounds were still clean. But she could also tell that much of his energy was being used to fight the infection.

"How is it that we have seen no trolls?" Sorrow asked Gazrak.

"All trolls but the oldest and youngest go to say farewell to the king. But soon, trolls will turn back, and those who guard the tunnels will come here," Gazrak answered.

"Does the Troll King fear invasion, that he keeps guards in these levels?" Ginger asked.

"The Troll King fears *humans* will discover Underth," Gazrak answered.

The ferrets cleared away the scraps from the meal, and Little Fur remembered the leaves the

owl had given her. She got them out and made sure the others rubbed the leaves into palm of paw and sole of foot before she attended to herself. The fragrance of the dried leaf was mild but distinctive; Little Fur could not see how it would hide the strong musk of fox and ferret, let alone her own scent.

They set off again, and came to another downward troll hole. This was also a natural fissure in the earth, but it had been worked and honed by burrowers. Little Fur smelled pain and cruelty and weariness in the smooth walls. She guessed that the trolls had forced animals to labor for them.

A little farther down, she was startled to see the flaking remnants of ancient carvings. They were not the work of any sort of creature Little Fur

126

knew, nor could she smell human on them. She asked Gazrak who had made them, and to her astonishment, he said that they were old troll work. Little Fur had always thought of trolls as primitive, yet the carvings proved there had been trolls who valued patience and beauty and skill. Perhaps her mother had been such a troll!

"Does earth magic flow in Underth?" Little Fur asked after a time, for although the earth magic now moved like near-freezing water, its flow was still strong.

"It is in Underth," Gazrak said, "but there are many places where it cannot go. The Troll King seeks to poison all of the city so that the earth spirit cannot pry into his domain."

The tunnel became steeper and less well kept, and in some sections, there had been cave-ins. The companions had to move carefully, lest they send an avalanche sliding down to warn of their descent. Ahead, Gazrak and Sorrow stopped often to sniff and listen.

As they walked, Little Fur's fear was left

behind. Her mind was completely occupied by the complexity of the earth about her. To her troll senses, it was as diverse and enchanting as the wilderness was to her elf senses.

At last, the tunnel flattened out and they came to a doorway carved into the rock. It was only after studying the intricate pattern carved into its frame that Little Fur noticed small luminous mushrooms growing thickly in damp patches along the edges of the tunnel. Her nose told her that they were poisonous, but her instinct told her that they were also valuable. So she broke off one of the toadstools and pushed it into the hem of her dress, where a clever pocket had been sewn.

Gazrak suddenly stiffened. "A troll comes," he said urgently.

"Is there a place to hide ahead, or must we turn back?" Sorrow asked.

"We should go on," said Gazrak, "and fast and quietly." They hurried to another crack and crept into it. Little Fur hoped that the Sett Owl had been right about the leaves hiding their scents.

It was not long before they heard the thud of heavy feet. Little Fur's elf blood surged with curiosity. Then came sounds like guttural voices. Little Fur thought Gazrak was mistaken about there being only one troll, but when the troll appeared, she saw that it was talking to itself. She could not understand its snarling language, and wondered how Shikra and Brave Kell would get the information they needed from the trolls.

The troll was enormous, with clublike arms hanging almost to the ground and a huge, bent body. The troll turned its head, and Little Fur pressed her fist into her mouth to silence a cry at the sight of its dreadful misshapen face. Its bald head grew out of its massive shoulders, and its nose was a lump of bristling flesh squeezed between two slitted eyes that gave off the same pallid radiance as the toadstool she had plucked.

Little Fur found it impossible to imagine that she was kin to this terrifying beast. Yet its ears, though many times bigger, were furled and pointed like hers, and like her, it had four great hairy toes and four fingers, but all ending in long, curving yellow claws. The worst thing about the troll, though, was the reek of its hatred, which flowed out from it like thick smoke from a fire.

The troll stopped right beside their hiding place. It muttered something in its rough language that sounded like a question. Then it began to sniff.

Little Fur held her breath.

But the troll merely stood sniffing and muttering for a time before shaking its head and continuing on its way.

CHAPTER 10
The Troll King's Domain

Little Fur and her companions hid from many trolls as they continued, all as dreadful-looking as the first, though not all as huge and hairy. Many were lean and hairless, like pale spiders, and ran upon all fours. Some smelled of illness, and aside from being filthy, many were covered in black sores. All bore bruises and grazes and cuts that spoke of their aggressive nature. But worst of all were their pale glowing eyes and the persistent reek of hatred.

For the first time, Little Fur understood why

those who knew of her parentage wondered at it. But none of the trolls that had passed them in the tunnels had been she-trolls, so maybe the females were less grotesque than their brothers. How could her father have loved her mother otherwise? Yet if all of the trolls that journeyed from Underth to the surface were male, how had her parents met? Little Fur shook these confusing questions out of her head.

The Sett Owl's leaves saved the travelers from being found, but almost all of the trolls that passed by their hiding places did stop to sniff long and curiously before going on their way.

They came to a strange chamber carved out of the rock, where the path they had been following split into several paths, each with its own opening. Like the carvings Little Fur had seen higher up, it was ancient troll work. Unlike the other chambers they had passed through, this one was not empty. The air flickered with blue sparks and flashes of light. It was not until Gazrak snarled and bit and whipped his long tail painfully about to drive her and the others out of the chamber that Little Fur realized she and the rest of them had fallen into a fascinated stupor.

"The sparks of light are glamours designed by the Troll King to catch intruders," the rat said irritably. "You must follow my orders, for I, Gazrak, am immune, like all those born within Underth."

They entered the next chamber warily, and found themselves in a heavy yellowish mist that made them all want to lie down and sleep. Again, Gazrak tormented them until they had passed safely out of the chamber and onto the correct path. Once outside the chambers, they felt the Troll King's magic fade quickly. They continued in this way, negotiating chambers and their illusions and hiding from trolls. Little Fur asked where the paths they did not take might lead, but Gazrak only muttered that they led to diggings and other trollish places.

The final chamber was more elaborate and less eroded than the others they had passed through.

Little Fur gazed at the intricate carvings covering the walls, feeling that the tiny pictures were a language that she might understand if she had enough time to study them.

"What is it?" Sorrow asked.

Little Fur turned to see Gazrak poised at one of the doors leading from the chamber, chewing his paws and sniffing. For the first time, the rat seemed uncertain.

Sorrow probed further when Gazrak made no response. "Do ye smell danger?"

"Something smells different," the rat said at last. He went to each of the doors leading from the chamber, including the one they had come through. He sniffed at one and then another, seeming ever more dissatisfied. At last, he stopped at one door.

"Are ye sure it is this way?" the fox asked, coming to stand beside him.

"This is the last chamber before the caverns of Underth," the rat muttered. "When Gazrak last

came through it, there was only one path." Again he began to step through the opening and again the fox stopped him.

"Give me your tail before ye go through."

The rat looked affronted, but when the fox's stare did not waver, he held out the frayed end of his long tail. Sorrow took it solemnly between his teeth, and Gazrak stepped out with a sneer. The rat gave a shrill scream as the path fell away under him. It had been a bridge of powdery sand. As with the glamours, once the trick had been revealed, it was easy to see that all but one of the roads leading out of the chamber would lead an unwary traveler to his or her death.

The only safe path lay farthest to the right, and it was Sorrow who led the way onto it. Gazrak was deeply shaken. When he took the lead again, he crept ahead, trembling with terror. Fortunately, they had not far to go before Little Fur noticed a greenish glow ahead.

"The light comes from the great subterranean

caverns where we will find the troll city of Underth," Gazrak explained.

Little Fur gasped in wonder at the vastness of the cavern visible from the end of the tunnel. If she had not known they were deep under the earth, she would have thought they had entered an open valley with a clouded night sky arching above, hiding the moon and stars. Greenish light glowed from behind a great range of high, jagged hills running in a wide curve from one side of the enormous cavern to the other. A path led from where they stood at the tunnel entrance, down the steeply sloping side of the cavern to the foot of the hills.

"We must not stand here where we can be seen," Sorrow said.

Gazrak darted sideways along the slanting wall of the cavern, his progress sending avalanches of black rock rattling down the slope. The rest of them toiled after him on the uneven, treacherous ground. They headed for some low, tumbled hillocks of rock and rubble that had fallen from the cavern walls.

Picking her way along, Little Fur saw that the high hills, like the mounds of black rock they were walking through, were enormous piles of sharp rock fragments. By the time the animals had reached the very beginning of the curving arm of high hills, all of them were black-streaked from slipping and stumbling. But Little Fur was sure-footed, thanks to her troll blood.

Gazrak permitted them a rest once they had gotten into the hills. They all sank down gratefully, too weary to care how hard or dirty the surface was. Ginger murmured that it was night in the overworld. Little Fur did not doubt it. Her own instincts were less attuned to the world they had left behind than to this black underworld of stone and shadow.

They had not rested long before Shikra rose, saying, "A journey soon begun is sooner ended."

Little Fur could smell that Gazrak did not like the she-ferret taking the lead, but the rest of them rose and set off again. There was nothing green or growing on the hills, but as with the earlier paths, earth magic ran slowly through and about the black stones. It was not the nearness of Underth

that slowed the flow of earth magic, but rather a natural sluggishness due to passing through dense stone and earth undisturbed by the burrows of small beasts or the roots of plants and trees.

The only movement in all that stony blackness was the occasional shift of stones, their own ghostly shadows running over the rocks before them and, a few times, a plume of steam from a tiny crack. Little Fur's troll blood told her the steam welled from deeper still in the earth, where rock was soft and hot. Perhaps there, she thought with a thrill of wonder, the earth spirit dwelt in a land of burning rivers of molten stone.

They had walked for hours when the fox suggested another stop. He smelled of weariness now, and Little Fur was about to add her plea to his, but Gazrak insisted they keep going. "Underth will be visible soon. Then we will see who has the courage to venture there," he said sourly.

Little Fur became aware of a distant roaring. It gradually became so loud that she could not make herself heard to ask the bad-tempered rat

what it was. Long before they reached the source of the noise, her nose told her there was water flowing ahead. She imagined a great subterranean stream, so she was shocked when they came to the top of a rise and she saw that the roaring came not from a river, but from a great cascade of water bursting from the wall of the cavern and plunging down to jagged rocks below.

The waterfall was many times greater than the tiny falling stream within the wilderness, but for a moment, Little Fur imagined herself sitting peacefully on its mossy bank, cooling her feet and waiting for patients.

She shivered, shaking off the sense that a cold shadow had passed over her, and let her eyes follow the roaring water. It fell from such a height that much of it was mist by the time it reached the black teeth of the rocks below. But there was still water enough to form a swift river that churned and surged, cutting a deep chasm in the stony floor of the cavern. The sight and sound of the waterfall and river were so compelling that it was a moment before Little Fur saw the first clear view of Underth.

CHAPTER 11

Underth!

The city of trolls lay on the far side of the stony black plain on the other side of the river. Though swathed in a luminous yellow-green mist, Underth looked so like a human city that Little Fur gasped. Then she saw that what she had taken for black high houses were actually rearing pinnacles of rock. Some were so tall that their tops were lost in the general blackness that concealed the cavern roof. Underth was built about these pillars and crawled partway up their sides, a wild black infestation of crooked buildings made from the rock they were standing on.

"That is where the Troll King lives," Gazrak said, pointing to a building between two stone pillars with its back against the nearest wall of the cavern. "What you see is only part of the Troll King's palace," he continued. "Many tunnels and chambers are cut into the rock behind and under it."

Little Fur shifted her attention to the narrow streets coiling about the palace. There was a slow movement along them, and seeing where she looked, Gazrak explained that trolls were still returning from saying farewell to their king.

"I smell humans," Sorrow announced suddenly, his lips drawn back in a snarl.

Gazrak glanced at the fox, a flicker of surprise in his red eyes. "No humans are here, but it is said by some that Underth is built on the bones of ancient human buildings swallowed up by the earth in the long ago. The king does not like that story. Those who tell it are whipped." He gave a cackling laugh and then flinched.

"How do we get across the river?" Sorrow asked.

"There is a fording place," Gazrak answered. "But water is now flowing deeply across it."

"Is there no bridge?" the fox asked.

Little Fur caught the sharp and surprising scent of Sorrow's fear. Perhaps, like her, he had once almost drowned. Because she was concentrating on the scent of the fox, Little Fur's nose also caught a hint of infection. But before she could suggest cleaning the fox's wounds, Gazrak pointed to the waterfall. "The only bridge runs behind that," he said.

"A bridge *behind* a waterfall?" Ginger said doubtfully.

Gazrak turned on him furiously and snarled, "You will see!" He scuttled on over the stones.

Ginger gave Little Fur a sideways look that glimmered with amusement. They walked along the tops of the rocky hills until they were close enough to see that a bridge did pass behind the falls. They toiled down an awkward path that brought them to the edge of the chasm, where the

river boiled and surged, sending up billowing veils of mist. They were close enough now to see that the bridge was cracked and badly eroded, as well as slick and shining wet. Sorrow shook his head and ordered Gazrak to lead them to the ford. The companions followed the rat along the bank to the place where a solid bed of stones had been placed across the river.

"When the ford was built, the water was not yet so high or strong," Gazrak said.

Sorrow dipped one red paw into the raging waters before backing away. "The current is so strong that any of us will be swept away and drowned," he said.

"I told you so," Gazrak said obnoxiously.

"We must use water bridge," Shikra said, sounding regretful rather than afraid.

Gazrak bared long yellow teeth at her.

Brave Kell produced a strong plaited vine. Before they approached the bridge, they tied the vine around themselves so that they were connected, one to the other, with the fox in the lead. Glancing over the edge of the bridge, Little Fur saw that one misstep would bring them all tumbling down onto the rocks, jagged and black as rotted fangs below.

The moment she stepped onto the bridge, her apprehension was swallowed up in wonder. Her troll senses told her that the bridge had once been intricately carved by the same trolls that had done the carvings she had seen on the way to Underth. Little Fur could not wait to tell Brownie the pony about them, to see if he had ever heard any stories of a fair age when trolls had valued carvings more than destruction.

For all her delight, Little Fur was soon longing to get off the bridge. The thunderous bellowing of the water hurt her ears, and the air was so wet that she was half drowned with the effort of trying to breathe. The crossing went on so long that at one point, Little Fur wondered if it was a magical bridge that would never end. Then suddenly they were stumbling from the end of it.

Little Fur wanted to rest, but Gazrak insisted they find a better place. He pointed to some low hills of black rock halfway between the city and the waterfall. "We must reach that spot before we can rest safely and make camp," he said.

By the time they had reached the hills, Little Fur was tired and numb with cold. But she became alert when the air grew suddenly deliciously warm. They had entered an area dotted with bubbling pools of mud. The veil of yellow-green mist that hung over Underth also rose thickly from the surface of the mud pools. Little Fur realized the troll city must have many such pools to give off such an intense light.

The rat guided them to a small area of dry ground in the midst of the mud. Little Fur sank gratefully down beside Ginger. She was asleep in a moment, unable to care if a whole company of trolls came marching along.

When she woke, the first thing Little Fur saw was Sorrow, sitting apart from the rest of them as he always did. She did not have to smell him to know that he had not slept. She slipped off her pouches and was relieved to find that they had kept her herbs dry.

Laying out what she needed, Little Fur prepared a fresh tisane for the fox. Once it was ready, she carried it to him, steeling herself for an argument, but he drank willingly enough, refusing only to let her cleanse the wounds again. When she tried to insist, he snapped at her, saying he wanted to scout out the track to the city.

Little Fur joined the others. Gazrak was asleep, but Ginger was awake and grooming himself, while the ferrets prepared food from their backpacks. Little Fur gave Shikra mushrooms and nuts from her pouch to season their meal. The ferret bowed as she accepted them.

"What made you and your brother volunteer for the expedition?" Little Fur asked curiously.

"Not volunteering. Great Mother send us to Sett Owl," Shikra answered in a soft, whispery voice.

"The Sett Owl asked your mother for help?" Little Fur asked.

The ferret chittered delicately with laughter. "Queen, whom us call Great Mother, sent us. Once Sett Owl long ago gave advice. Shikra knowing not what it was, but Great Mother say she owe debt to Sett Owl. If Mother owe debt, then children pay. So each year, she send two young ferrets to Sett Owl to see if anything needful."

"Never was any of Mother's children given such great and important task as us," Brave Kell added solemnly.

"Didn't your own mother mind that this . . . this expedition might be dangerous?" Little Fur asked.

"Someone must do. Why not us? Are us more valuable than other things that live?" Brave Kell laughed. "Little Mother say us must serve Great Mother and Sett Owl with honor." He glanced at his sister. "If us succeed, us be heroes."

"Great Mother say us not to think of heroing," Shikra scolded. "She say, 'Be brave but also wise. Hero only brave.'"

The conversation was interrupted by the fox's return. He announced that when they had finished their food, he and Ginger would carry the ferrets as close as they dared to the outer edge of Underth so they could begin their spying. Then he took his food a few steps away to eat by himself. Ginger came to sit by Little Fur. She stroked his soft coat, taking comfort from it, and wished there was something more nourishing for him

to eat than the bit of crust he gnawed. When she said so, Ginger murmured that it didn't matter, for there would be mice and cockroaches in the city.

152

"But *you* must not go into the city!" she said, horrified.

"There are cats in Underth," Ginger rumbled.

Little Fur wondered how he knew that, but she wanted to listen to the conversation Sorrow was having with Gazrak.

"Which way did the Troll King go out of this cavern?" the fox asked.

"The entrance to the under-road is on the other side of the great cavern," Gazrak answered. "To reach it from within the palace, the Troll King would have used Kingsbridge, which begins within the palace, passes over the city and the river and ends at the entrance to the under-road. All trolls who went with the Troll King to see him off would have marched with him on Kingsbridge. But when they return to Underth, they must use Lessbridge, for none may walk Kingsbridge without the king. If we had taken the path we saw leading to the hills when first we entered the great cavern, it would have brought us to Lessbridge."

"Perhaps we can use Lessbridge when it is

time for us to leave, rather than the water bridge," Sorrow said.

"*You* may travel that way, fox," the rat sneered. "On it you will find the end you seek. But I will use the water bridge, for *I* wish to live."

The fox merely looked at Ginger and nodded, then told the ferrets to climb onto their backs. As they left, the fox cast Little Fur a strangely pointed look and said, "Stay here with the food, Healer."

Little Fur clambered to the top of the nearest mound of stones so that she could see Ginger, Sorrow, Shikra and Brave Kell enter the city. She was startled at how much more she could see of Underth. The façade and ramparts of the Troll King's palace were clearly visible now, as well as the open square before its gates. She could even see Kingsbridge arching away from it on the other side.

Fox and cat flowed over the black stone plain and vanished into another cloud of luminous yellow-green mist that hung over a tumble of black boulders close to the edge of the city. Once they had gone out of sight, Little Fur watched to see if she could spot the ferrets entering the city, but they were invisible. After a long moment, she gave up. Heaving a sigh, she turned to climb back down to their camp, only to see Gazrak picking and pulling at one of the tiny ferret packs, trying to get at their meager supply of food.

"You greedy thing!" she cried without thinking.

After a stunned glance at her, Gazrak fled, dragging the pack with him. Little Fur dared not shout again, and she turned back to the city, terrified that her cry would bring trolls to investigate.

"I am sorry," Little Fur said later.

Sorrow had returned alone, leaving Ginger stationed among some boulders to watch for the ferrets.

Sorrow shrugged. "It can't be helped. And it may be that the rat's disappearance is the betrayal

155

the Sett Owl foresaw. If that is so, we can be glad it is so small a betrayal."

"But how will we get back to the overworld?" she asked.

"I can sniff the way, now that I know where and what the dangers are," Sorrow said.

"Do you think Gazrak has run away for good?"

"For good or ill, he has gone," the fox answered. "Now we must find a better place to make camp. I want to be able to see the city at all times."

Once they had found a place that suited him, Sorrow wanted to look for Gazrak, but Little Fur insisted on being allowed to cleanse his wounds. He gave a terse sigh and submitted. She washed the two gashes on his flank, noting that they were red and unhealthy-looking. There was nothing wrong with the stitches she had made, but the fox's spirit was not letting the wounds heal.

"Tell me of the dog," Sorrow demanded.

Realizing he wanted to be distracted, she described the one-eyed cat Sly and her encounter with the dog behind its web of metal. "I could smell that Sly liked it that the dog was hurt," Little Fur said, remembering how this had shocked her.

"Some creatures are like that," Sorrow answered. "It is in their nature to walk the edges between things like safety and danger, pleasure and pain. It is the balancing they like, rather than one thing or the other."

"Why do you suppose the humans were hunting the dog?" Little Fur asked.

"Humans do not like to lose the things they regard as their own." The bleakness in his eyes had leaked into his voice.

"You don't like humans much, do you?" Little Fur asked.

"There is nothing to like in them," the fox said coldly.

Little Fur said softly, "I thought that once, too. I believed that humans were as ill-intentioned as trolls, loving nothing better than hurting and killing things. But . . . many of them do not smell of hatred and cruelty. Some smell of wonder and kindness, and when they sing, it is so beautiful that they drive away the darkness in themselves."

"There is nothing good in humans," the fox snarled. "If ye think there is, ye are a fool. If ever ye were in the hands of a human, ye would soon discover that this one-eyed cat's cruelty was nothing beside the cruelty of humans."

Suddenly the clangor of bells filled the air. The fox was up in a flash, running to where he could see the city. Little Fur followed, her heart shuddering at the thought that the ferrets had been caught.

"Now we miss the rat, for he could have told us what the bells mean," Sorrow muttered.

"Where do you think he went?" Little Fur asked.

"Not into the city," Sorrow said. "Gazrak feared coming to Underth. He stank of it. If he is not still here and hiding somewhere about us in these stony hills, he is headed for the surface."

CHAPTER 12
A Bottle of Sickness

Sorrow searched for Gazrak while Little Fur kept watch. But there were no more bells, and there was no sign of trolls moving beyond the edge of their city. When Sorrow returned, he wearily told Little Fur that he hadn't found any trace of the rat. He cast himself down and slept briefly, then rose and went to relieve Ginger, refusing the food Little Fur had prepared.

Little Fur did not insist that he eat, or tell him he ought to have rested longer, for his mood seemed darker than ever. After he had gone, she slept fitfully and dreamed the Old Ones were calling her. When she woke, it was with the distinct feeling that it was Crow who had been calling.

She sat up, stretched, and found Ginger curled beside her. He stirred as she prepared them a scanty meal. "Did you see anything to explain the bells?" she asked.

"No," the cat replied. "But I do not think they signaled the capture of the ferrets." He paused and then added, "I also do not believe that Gazrak's disappearance means the rat is the betrayer the Sett Owl warned us of."

"The betrayer had to come because it was needed, and we needed Gazrak to guide us to Underth," Little Fur said.

"I do not know if running away can be called a betrayal," Ginger said. "Perhaps the rat was merely frightened away by your shout."

Little Fur flushed. Her troll blood was affecting her in ways other than improving her ability to sense the nature of earth and rock. Suspicion and doubt were part of her trollness, for a troll would need such instincts to survive among other trolls. They were less of an evil than they were a necessity. Little Fur wondered what else she would come to learn about herself before this journey was over.

Ginger ate and curled up to sleep again, asking her to awaken him in an hour. Little Fur wanted to lie down with him but feared that she would sleep too deeply, so she sat by him and studied the troll city, wondering where Shikra and Brave Kell were and whether they were safe. She decided that it was harder to wait for someone who was in danger than to be the one facing the danger.

Ginger woke less gracefully than usual at Little Fur's touch. For a moment he stared at her, his orange eyes clouded by sleep. Then he said, "I dreamed that Crow was calling for me. . . ."

Little Fur gasped. "I dreamed of Crow, too."

Ginger stretched. "No doubt his heart aches for us as well."

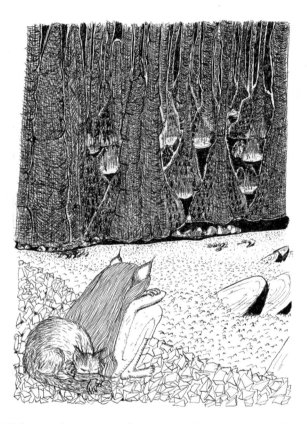

When she was alone, Little Fur set about
preparing another tisane for the fox, puzzling
over how she might convince him to let her try
to heal his spirit. When she heard a sound behind
her, she turned to present him with her carefully

thought-out argument—only to find it was Ginger.

"Sorrow is gone," he said, smelling of concern. "His scent trail leads to the city."

Little Fur felt a sick sense of things going wrong. "Maybe Shikra and Kell came to get him."

"I will follow his scent trail, but you must come with me and wait in case the ferrets return while I am gone," Ginger said.

It took them twenty minutes to reach the spot the fox had chosen as a rendezvous for the spies. It was a good hiding place, because a concealing haze of bright steam rose from pools of bubbling mud. Ginger slipped into the city like a gray shadow, and Little Fur sat down to wait. She was close enough now to see that all of Underth was built upon a great slab of natural rock. That explained why the city had such an abrupt edge. No doubt the black stones were too unstable to build on. The troll dwellings looked even less impressive close up, constructed of more black stones carelessly mortared together with mud.

Trolls passed up and down a street that ran for a short way along the very edge of the city. Some were as misshapen as those in the tunnels, but others were much smaller and finer. Like Little Fur, they had long hair, and though it was hard to tell, she thought they might be she-trolls.

As time passed without any sign of the others, her unease grew. What ought she to do if none of them returned? Must she try to complete the quest on her own? But how could she? Even if she managed to creep into the city unnoticed and get the information the Sett Owl needed, could she bypass the Troll King's glamours to get back to the surface?

The distinct sound of rocks clicking softly together cut into her thoughts. She looked up to see Ginger unraveling himself from cat shadow. To her amazement, the one-eyed cat Sly was with him! Only then did she remember that the black dog had spoken of tracking Sly to the troll hole.

"Greetings, Little Fur," Sly said in her purring voice, her single green eye as bright as a jewel

164

against her sleek black coat. Her long tail twitched, its broken tip the only awkward part of her.

"Sly! I am glad to see you, but how do you come to be here?" Little Fur asked, reaching out to stroke the silky pelt.

"I come here from time to time because it amuses me," Sly said lightly. "I was surprised to find Ginger's scent. I thought I must be wrong until I came upon him blundering around." Her eye glimmered with amused malice.

Ginger only licked at his paw and said, "Gazrak must have signaled the fox from the edge of the city. I picked up his scent soon after I entered the outskirts."

"But why would Gazrak go into the city, and why call Sorrow in?" Little Fur asked.

"The ferrets have not come back?" Ginger asked.

Little Fur shook her head worriedly.

Ginger's orange eyes narrowed. "Then I will return to Underth," he said. "I will go into the palace, where the scents of Sorrow and Gazrak lead, for it may be that they are all in danger."

Sly coiled around the gray cat, her green eye seeming to laugh. "If a fox and a rat went to the palace, the fox, at least, is a prisoner. And you cannot venture there, Ginger, for the Troll King's glamours would see you captured, even were you shrouded in cat shadow. Unless you allow me to help you. We can seek the stink of fox and ferret together. The aroma of rat will be there in abundance, for many rats serve the Troll King."

Something was troubling Little Fur. "Sly, we rubbed special leaves on our feet to cover our scent. How can you smell Ginger, and how could Ginger have smelled the fox or the ferrets?"

"I do not know about any leaves," Sly said, sounding bored.

"I do not know either, but I could smell both the fox and the ferrets," Ginger said.

After the two cats had gone, Little Fur thought about the leaves the Sett Owl had given them, and wondered if the scent could be wearing off. She had not thought to ask the owl if they must be rubbed on repeatedly. She wished she had at least applied some to Ginger's paws.

Weary hours passed. She saw many trolls, both the great lumbering kind and the thin, snaky sort. But she also saw several trolls that walked upright and were slender, with long hair like hers. Now she was certain that they were she-trolls. Sometimes small trolls accompanied them.

Finally, worn down by useless worry, Little Fur decided to enter the city herself. She could pass for a troll child if she dirtied herself and walked with her shoulders hunched. She took off her tunic and hid it with the remaining backpack. Then she hung her pouch of herbs and the green stone her mother had left her beneath her under-shift. Last of all, she tore the sleeves and hem of her dress and smeared mud into her hair to dull its brightness.

Suddenly Shikra appeared, racing over the jagged stones to the boulders and bubbling mud. She flung herself into Little Fur's arms, trembling violently. Little Fur held her gently and looked her over for serious injury, but found none. Still, fear itself was a deeper kind of wounding. The healer bathed the burnt and ruffled ferret gently, using water from her bottle. She could smell that the burns stung. At last, Shikra sat up on her hind legs and composed herself.

"Us hear troll speak of meeting in palace. Us follow troll. He go in palace, then Brave Kell make diversion," she reported. "When bells ring, troll guards run from posts and us slip inside, too. Inside, no troll looking properly at us. Maybe they think no one can get inside palace. Or maybe they think us rats. Or maybe some ferrets serve Troll King."

"What happened in the meeting room?" Little Fur prompted.

"Long argument," Shikra said. "Trolls argue about which troll in control while Troll King away. If something happen to king, whoever in charge becomes king. Big troll say he is master while master away. Brod is name. He say his blood same as Troll King's blood. He say Brod perform great service for king in carrying sickness of cats to human city. Us not know if what he say *true*. Impossible to smell if troll lie or not,

169

for much they say is nonsense they think true."

"Did they say why the Troll King wanted to make cats sick?" Little Fur asked.

Shikra said, "Trolls speak of experiment and of animal called Indyk and of king's plan to destroy earth spirit." She hesitated. "Trolls also speak of . . . Little Fur."

Little Fur stared at her in astonishment. "A troll said *my* name?"

"Brod say Little Fur most bitter enemy of Troll King. King want . . ." She stopped.

"He wants to kill me," Little Fur whispered.

"Brod say Little Fur ruin Troll King's last plan and work against him each day of living," Shikra said. "But when trolls speak of killing earth spirit, they speak of Indyk and of cat sickness."

"What is an indyk?" Little Fur murmured, tasting the strange word and finding no flavor she recognized. She shook her head and asked, "What happened to you and Brave Kell?"

Shikra shuddered deeply again. "After talking, another fight. Shikra and Brave Kell creep away, but rats outside the chamber in hall smell us spies. Us taken prisoner. Us carried down many stairs into vast chamber where are many cages. All creatures in them smell of fear and sickness and pain. Us very frightened. They put us in cage. Bird in next cage scream that Troll King will hurt us to make us sing song of pain. Bird say human taught song to Troll King. Bird smelled of madness but also of truth."

Little Fur asked, "How did you get away?"

"Gazrak and Sorrow come. Rat gnawed cage binding so Shikra and Brave Kell free. Other animals scream and cry and beg: *Free! Free us!* Noise bring troll guard, then another. Sorrow commands: *Ferrets, go before more come. Do not look back. Find healer and flee.* Then Sorrow attack troll."

"Then what happened?" Little Fur cried, breathless.

"Shikra obey Sorrow. But Brave Kell being hero! Troll strike him hard. Kell hit wall of cavern with terrible crunch. *Shikra cannot feel mind*

171

anymore! Shikra want to go where brother lying, but Gazrak scream: *Follow!* Shikra obey." This last was uttered with a heart-rending sob.

"Shikra, do you know what happened to Sorrow? Was he . . . ?" She found she could not say the word.

"Not know," Shikra cried. "Gazrak led Shikra to crack in wall. Crack bring us to passage close to door leading out of palace, but there stand guards. Gazrak order Shikra wait until guards gone, then run. Then rat go running to troll. He crying out that intruders are in palace. When they gone, Shikra run. Not knowing what happened to Gazrak. Shikra never see brother again. . . ." She wept, and Little Fur could not comfort her.

An hour passed, and a hard and terrible hour it was for Little Fur. Shikra fell into a restless, whimpering sleep. Little Fur was thinking again of going into the city when suddenly Ginger appeared from around the boulders with Gazrak scuttling by his side. The cat carried the limp form of Brave Kell in his mouth. He laid the ferret very gently at Little Fur's feet. Smelling her brother, Shikra woke and gave a cry, but Little Fur hushed her, promising that her brother was not dead. He was unconscious and badly bruised, but his worst injury was a broken leg.

Little Fur washed Brave Kell's wounds and treated them, and all the time he slept. She bade his sister cuddle up to him. The need to care for her injured brother steadied Shikra, and their bond would help to mend both of their spirits.

Only when the two were settled did she question Ginger, who explained that he and Sly had entered the palace by an obscure door, and had hidden, mantled in cat shadow, until they had heard enough to know that intruders had been captured. Sly knew where they would be taken, and they had gone there, only to find Gazrak sniffing at the unconscious Kell.

"Sorrow . . ."

"Sorrow was caged and badly hurt," Ginger said. "We tried to open his cage, but the knot was too strong. He said that he did not fear to die. He commanded us to take Kell and leave Underth with you. He said the trolls were terrified of what their king would say when he learned that spies had entered the city in his absence, and very soon they would begin to scour the city for intruders. Sorrow said Gazrak must go, too, for the trolls know him."

"It is already too late to use the tunnel," Gazrak said suddenly.

"What do you think we should do, then?" Little Fur asked him.

"We must use the under-road," Gazrak said.

"But that is the way the Troll King and his warriors will return," Little Fur protested.

"We have only to travel on the under-road to places where the earth is cracked and there are narrow paths leading to the surface," Gazrak said eagerly.

Brave Kell groaned and opened his eyes. He saw Shikra bending over him and murmured, "Kell was a fool."

"Brave Kell," she whispered, taking his paw and nibbling it tenderly.

"Wise Shikra," he answered softly, and rubbed his head against her. Then he grimaced. "Ugh, leg hurts."

Little Fur asked Ginger what had happened to Sly. She half expected that he would tell her the one-eyed cat had vanished again, but to her great surprise he said, "It was hard to carry the ferret swiftly without hurting him further, and my cat shadow would not cover him. Sly ran out of the gates and made the guards chase her so that I could slip out unnoticed with Gazrak and Kell."

"The guards will come back," Gazrak warned miserably. "We are all doomed."

Little Fur could smell that the others were looking to her to decide what they should do. "Listen," she said, trying to sound stern and calm. And then she told them her plan.

"That is not what the fox ordered," Ginger said mildly.

"Sorrow no longer leads us," Little Fur answered. "I do. All of you must take the underroad. Before you go, a trail must be laid to draw the trolls after you. It must be laid so that they will not discover where it leads too swiftly."

"What will you do?" Ginger asked.

"I will enter the city disguised as a troll child to learn more of the Troll King's plans for the earth spirit. And I will try to free Sorrow."

"How will Little Fur escape from Underth?" Shikra asked.

"I will go out the same way we came in, for the trolls who guard that way will have followed you."

"If we would go, we must go *now*!" Gazrak said urgently.

Little Fur nodded, her eyes on Ginger, for despite his silence, she knew he was the one she had to convince. "You have to go, because Brave Kell cannot walk and you must carry him," she said gently.

The gray cat gave a soft sigh that smelled of surrender, and said very softly, "I do not want to leave you here."

"Neither did Crow want us to leave him, yet we left because it was needful."

Ginger lowered his head and Little Fur put her arms around him.

CHAPTER 13
Little Fur Alone

Brave Kell rode on Ginger's back, and Gazrak and Shikra flanked the gray cat as they departed. Little Fur longed to call out to them to stop, to say that she had changed her mind, that she was too small and not made for the task of spying. But the voice in her deepest soul spoke not of fear or longing, but of what was right and what was wrong. So she mastered herself and let them go.

Hours passed before Little Fur heard the bells that signaled the trolls had found the trail. Little Fur gathered her courage and made her way to

179

the edge of the city. The moment she stepped onto the great slab of rock upon which the city was built, she felt earth magic pulsing through it.

She hunched her shoulders to make her neck short, and bent her legs to achieve a rolling gait. She made her way along the street she had watched for so long and, turning the corner, entered a wider street. Pools of bubbling mud were everywhere, hung with veils of the shining mist that lit the city. Little Fur had spied out a route to the palace, but there was no need to keep to it, for the building was clearly visible between the stone pillars.

Suddenly a great host of trolls came thundering toward her along the street carrying clubs and spears. Little Fur froze. But the trolls did not look at her as they passed. She was not alone as she continued to thread her way in the direction of the palace. Older trolls and she-trolls, some of them attended by thin, crouching trolls who seemed like servants, were headed the same way. From what she could smell of the conversations around her, they were wondering what was going on.

As she reached the edge of the square, a pain made her double over. She knew at once what it was: Ginger was going away from her. She made herself stand up straight and ignore it, knowing it was only a matter of time before it would pass, as the pull toward Crow had done.

The square was very bright from many pools of bubbling mud. It was also busy, with trolls arriving and more trolls pushing carts of cooked food that other trolls were buying. Troll children ran about, throwing mud balls at one another.

Little Fur made her way to a wall where a number of older trolls squatted, picking their teeth or dozing in the warmth thrown out by the nearby mud pools. Sitting beside them, she half closed her eyes as if she, too, were sleepy.

Little Fur studied the façade of the Troll King's palace. Seen this close, the whole city was even more like a human city, with straight lines and sharp angles. Perhaps this palace was something left over from the humans, something which trolls had taken for their own. Her troll senses assured her that much of what was deep under the earth had once been on the surface, and much that now lay in the sun had been born deep in the earth.

The palace's two enormous entrance doors stood open and were guarded by four great shaggy trolls. Armed with spears whose ends glimmered sharp and silver, they were very alert and glared about ferociously. There were two smaller doors to one side of the building. One was shut fast, and a single guard was stationed before the other, which was ajar. But he was also alert and carried a spear at the ready.

Little Fur waited to see what the guards did when someone entered the palace, but no one came or went. She tried again to understand what the trolls were saying, but other than smelling the seriousness in their words, she could make no sense of their language. Her only chance to learn more of the Troll King's plans lay in rescuing Sorrow, who might have learned more during his imprisonment.

No bright and clever idea formed itself in her tired mind. Little Fur felt like weeping at her stupidity for thinking she could make such a daring rescue. She understood that this despair arose from her elf blood, which longed for the sky and the sunlight, but the troll part of her was stubborn. Whether or not she despaired, she *would* find a way to get to the fox and free him.

Incredibly, she slept, and her sleep was fitful and full of nightmares. She dreamed that the Troll King sent an army of trolls to burn the beaked house. That changed into a dream of Sly being stroked by the huge horny hands of the Troll King; and then of Sorrow, ringed by fire, beyond which she saw humans jeering and laughing at his terror.

She woke to the gnawing pain that told her Ginger was getting farther and farther away. She did not understand why the pain of separation was not fading, as it had done with Crow. She was about to rise when a great troop of troll guards thundered into the square.

A huge troll lumbered from the palace gates to meet them. The other trolls bowed, and she smelled his name in their mutters. *Brod!* Shikra had said this was the troll who had assumed leadership in the absence of the king. His roars smelled of questions, but when one of the other trolls began to speak, Brod gave a bellow of rage and struck him a savage blow that laid him unconscious. Then he began to roar at the troll warriors. Little Fur could make nothing of his words, but she guessed he had been told that the intruders had gotten out of the subterranean caverns.

One of the troll warriors handed a scrap of cloth to Brod. It was the material Ginger had used to lay a winding trail to the under-road! Brod sniffed at the cloth, then uttered a sharp command. The troll warriors turned and went thundering out of the square. Little Fur could only guess that Brod had dispatched them to search along the under-road.

Once the guards had marched away, Brod went back inside. The trolls remaining in the square clustered together, grunting and growling and waving their huge hairy arms at one another. To her surprise, Little Fur was able to understand some of their words. They were discussing the spies, wondering how they had the courage to go along the under-road, where they were sure to encounter the returning Troll King. One troll said that the spies couldn't know the king had gone that way, and what a horrible surprise that would be for them. A knot of trolls began to argue about what the spies wanted, anyway, and who had sent them.

Little Fur's ears pricked up when it sounded like one of the trolls was speaking of a spy that had been killed, but before she could hear more, they shuffled away. She turned her attention back to the palace gates, wishing she had asked

Shikra what Brave Kell had done to cause a diversion. Since she had not, she had better walk around the side of the palace to see if there was another way in.

She was about to rise when—"Little Fur is very foolish to come here," a familiar purring voice said. Little Fur turned to find Sly beside her. The narrow black cat had not a shred of cat shadow about her, and yet so dark was her pelt that she blended perfectly into the troll city.

"What happened to you?" Little Fur asked her.

"I led the trolls away," she said smugly. "But why have you not escaped? Are the others still here?"

Was it Little Fur's imagination, or did Sly smell of anxiety? "The others have escaped along the under-road; I stayed to free Sorrow." Little Fur hesitated. "Can you help me get inside the palace?"

"Ginger told me that the fox wished to die."

"Sorrow's spirit is sick. If it were healed, I do

not believe he would want to die," Little Fur said. "Besides, it might be that Sorrow has learned something of the Troll King's plans, and that is what we came to discover."

Sly considered this, her green eye inscrutable. "I will help you to get to the fox. Wait here."

Little Fur watched her go, wishing Sly had told her what she meant to do.

Bells began clanging again, and trolls poured from the gates of the palace. As they rushed out into the square, the gate guards joined them. Little Fur readied herself to hurry to the unguarded entrance. Then she realized that the troll warriors were rushing toward *her*! She shrank back against the wall and made herself as inconspicuous as she could. But they surrounded her, and a troll said, "This is it. Ugh, smell! Elf blood."

One troll grabbed her wrist, but an older troll batted his hand away. "Master says she must walk to death on her own two feet."

Little Fur stumbled between the trolls to the palace gates, her head ringing with the stench of her captors. The trolls led her deep into the palace, which was filled with endless dank passages that had cavernous empty rooms on both sides. Little Fur had the impression that the palace was empty but for a few inhabitants. Maybe all who normally dwelt here were with their king. Her thoughts were clear but strangely cold, as if her emotions had frozen inside her.

Eventually, the trolls led her down a flight of steps that gradually wound into a tight spiral. The walls streamed with mineral-scented water and were slippery with algae that grew in great clusters on the luminous toadstools. For a moment, the flow of earth magic quickened under her feet, and Little Fur thought she heard the voice of the earth spirit whispering to her to have faith.

Sly must have been caught and questioned by the trolls. How else could they have found her so swiftly? Little Fur could not bear to think of the lean, clever cat brought low in trying to help her.

Down and down they went, until they came to an enormous door carved with more of the ancient troll symbols. One of the trolls pushed at the door with a grunt, and it swung inward. A dreadful smell of pain and fear and anguish flowed out, and Little Fur's steps faltered.

Another troll gave her a shove that sent her reeling through the door, and she heard him hiss that she was not to be harmed . . . for the moment.

CHAPTER 14
The Secrets of Sorrow

The nearly circular chamber Little Fur found herself in was a natural cave, empty but for a rough semicircle of cages of varying sizes set one atop the other. Little Fur stopped, her heart quailing, but the troll behind her forced her into one of the larger cages. She had to crawl over fouled rock to enter it, but at least it was a lower cage that rested on the rock, so she was not sundered from the earth spirit.

Again, very faintly, she seemed to hear the

voice of the earth spirit bidding her to have faith. *But have faith in what?* she wondered.

Her captors muttered to one another, and Little Fur tried to listen, but she was too frightened to concentrate. For a time, she knew nothing. Perhaps she fainted or fell into some dark dream, but when she came to her senses, she could hear the sounds of animals and birds. She crept to the bars of her cage and peered out.

The troll guards had all gone, though the reek of troll was all about her. She groped for the cage binding and found a great greasy knot that her fingers could not undo. Well, she could hardly have expected that it would be a simple knot she could untie. She began sniffing delicately, sifting through the awful odors. She could not find Sly's scent, but she found another she knew very well.

The smell of Sorrow.

He was alive but fevered, and his old wounds, and new ones, were so full of corruption that even were they safe within the grove of the Old Ones,

she would have had little hope of saving him.

"Ye should not have come." The voice of the fox whispered through the awful air.

"The others have all gotten safely away," she told him, trying to make her voice cheerful. "That was your doing. Shikra and Brave Kell told me how you saved them."

"I saved no one. I sought death coming here, and soon I will find it."

"I don't believe that was why you fought the trolls," Little Fur said. "I think you were trying to help the others to escape."

There was silence. Little Fur sniffed and could not tell if the fox slept or lay awake or in a delirium. At last he said, "I did not tell the troll Brod anything."

"Of course you didn't," Little Fur said. "My getting caught was a stupid mistake and all my own fault. I fear for Sly, because she was trying to help."

"The others left and ye stayed?" the fox asked.

"I made them go. I had to try to free you. And I need to learn more about the Troll King's plans."

There was a shudder of sound so close to a

moan that it took Little Fur several seconds to recognize it as bleak laughter. "The Troll King thinks ye are the earth spirit's chosen warrior. Perhaps he is right."

"I am a healer, not a warrior," Little Fur said gently. "I wish I could have healed you properly. Your spirit—"

"My spirit is what it is," the fox said. "And soon it will be free. As will yours, for I think ye will not long bear the greedy cruelty of Brod."

"You survived his questions," Little Fur said.

Again the shudder of laughter. "I can resist any pain," Sorrow said. "It is life that I cannot bear, this life in which there are things that can love the pain of other living things."

"What caused all of your wounds?" Little Fur asked. As she spoke, she understood something more. "Who hurt you and then healed your body so that you came to loathe the touch of a healer as if it were the touch of the one who injured you?"

The fox gave a light, eerie laugh. "I have always hated curiosity, but perhaps curiosity can also be a kind of courage."

"I am not courageous. I am very frightened," Little Fur whispered, and her voice shook.

"Hush," the fox said. "Listen: I remember my birth. I was born inside a machine. I opened my

nose and senses into a world of metal and wires and the smell of humans. The humans were the only warm things that smelled of life, and so I yearned for them. When they touched me, I licked at their hands, but they wore strange coverings that would not let me taste their scents. I longed for pack, and humans were the closest thing to pack I had, and so I strove to bond with them. But their scents did not mingle or strive toward mine. I was puzzled and began to doubt what I was and what I longed for.

"Then there came a human that touched me with bare hands and stroked my pelt. His skin took my scent and we were pack. I was content, and my mind strove toward the human. In time, I came to love him, for there was nothing else to love.

"But then he began to hurt me. Small hurts to begin with, that I thought must be accidents. My instincts told me that such accidents could happen among those who were pack, for pain is not separate from love. So I accepted the pain. The hurts grew worse, but each time, the human that I had come to think of as brother healed me. I sniffed for his regret or even for guilt, but there was nothing. The hurts grew even worse. There were machines that made sky-fire run through me. I sniffed for love and understood there was no smell of it in the human.

"Sometimes I was put into water and made to swim and swim until there was no strength in me, and then I drowned, but the human healed me. I was burnt, and the human healed me. I began to hate the human and to fear him, but the human did not hate any more than he loved. It was as if I were dead in his hands. He smelled of nothing I could understand. But I made it my quest to learn what he did feel. To understand.

"Then, one day, it came to me what I could smell on the human when he was hurting me. He was hurting me with sky-fire, and I smelled that he was interested in the hurting and what it caused me to do. He liked watching how I acted. He was curious about what I would do next.

198

"For the first time, I thought about escape. Beyond the machine, there was something that I smelled which called to my senses. I began to watch, and I saw that the humans in their white coats came and left the machine through a hole they closed behind them. A door. The smell that called me was beyond that door. So I plotted and thought, and I made a plan. Whenever the humans had hurt me badly, they put me onto a white bed and made me sleep and healed me. The bed was by the door.

"The next time they hurt me and put me there, I fought the sleep. I fought it just as I fought for hours not to drown and fought the sky-fire that swarmed through my bones and gnawed at them. I fought the sleep and I pretended sleep. The pain was terrible, but I was not afraid of pain. And when they were not watching because they thought I slept, I rolled and fell to the floor. I had never been on the floor before. It smelled of nothing. I was hurt but made myself walk. When a human entered, I crept out the door. I entered a long room where there was nothing but many more doors.

"Then one door opened as I sniffed, and the smell that flowed through it was very strong and urged me to come to it. The human who had opened the door saw me. I knew that I had just a second. So I hurled myself toward the gap. The human tried to shut the door, but I was in it, and although something tore open the wounds that had just been healed, I was outside of the machine. Seeing the sky for the first time and feeling the grass under my paws, I was overwhelmed. I might have stood there like that in a stupor of wonder until they caught me.

"But then I heard the voice of the human who had taught me pain. He held out his hand, and his voice was soft, as it had been when I loved him. Part of me wanted to go to him, as if all the pain had been a mistake. But then I saw him make the gesture that he made when he wanted other humans to hurt me. Behind him, a door had opened in the high metal web that ran all around the machine, and two men were coming through it toward me.

"I leaped at them. They had not expected it and tangled themselves trying to stop me. The wounds in me were torn further by that leap, but I passed through that gate and I was free."

Little Fur waited, crouched in her cage, hardly breathing, to hear what the fox would say next. But when she sniffed, she realized that the fox had fallen into a feverish sleep. She did not call out and awaken him to tell her more, for what end could there be except the one she would now share with him? The rest was clear enough anyway. He had escaped and realized that this freedom, and all the wild world that ought to have been his, had been stolen from him. There was no point in seeking other foxes, because he was not a fox in anything but shape. He was what the humans and the machine had made of him.

Sorrow.

Little Fur found that she was crying, and for a time she gave herself up to a sadness so profound that even her fear of the trolls and what they would do to her was swallowed up. She thought of the poor tiny fox cub Sorrow had been, born amidst humans in a machine instead of in a litter of cubs with a mother to suckle him. How had they managed it? And yet perhaps there was nothing humans could not do because there was nothing they *would* not do.

The sound of a door clanging and the thud of troll feet brought her back to an awareness of her own fate. It was the troll Brod, and his huge face was lit with greed and eager cruelty. She told herself that what she must now face was a small thing compared to what Sorrow had endured.

But she was wrong.

For walking with sleek black grace at the side of the huge troll was Sly.

CHAPTER 15
A Gift for the Troll King

Brod leaned over with a grunt and peered through the bars of the cage at Little Fur. His huge nostrils quivered, and a foul gust of air wafted at her through his thick, wet lips. The troll reached for the ropes that tied the cage door.

"Do you think that wise, Master?" It was Sly's voice, delicate and amused and full of malice.

The troll turned to her with a growl of irritation. "Wise? What you are saying?" he grunted.

"It is only that the Troll King himself might wish to have the pleasure of giving pain to one so important. He might be angry at the troll who usurped that pleasure."

"Important? This only one of spies. Maybe least of them because others left it behind," the troll snarled.

"Ahh, but it was not left behind, Master. It commanded the others to go, for this is their leader."

"Fox is leader." The troll glanced at the cage where Sorrow lay.

"The fox is nothing next to this one," Sly said eagerly. She shifted her green eye to Sorrow's cage, and her tone was disparaging. "That is why it could tell nothing. I think it will die before the king returns, and it may not please him that he cannot ask questions of it himself."

"Hah," the troll grunted. "Fox should not have resisted Brod. Maybe Brod would stop sooner if fox beg. But fox dare say no to Brod."

"He was a fool, Master. But he is only a fox," Sly said. "You need not fear the wrath of the king, for you will offer him this prize instead."

"What prize?" the troll demanded, aiming a slap of impatience at the cat.

Sly eluded the blow and rubbed her sleekness against his thick ankle. "You have captured Little Fur," she said. "Little Fur the healer, whom the king loathes above all other things except the earth spirit."

The troll looked as shocked as Little Fur felt at hearing Sly's words. He swung to squint at her. "*This* Little Fur? The great warrior?"

"Not all things that are great are large," Sly said.

The troll tugged at his huge lower lip. "If this Little Fur, king will be pleased."

"Brod is too modest!" Sly cried. "The king will shower the troll who caught Little Fur with gifts. He will proclaim to all that Brod is his heir and his favorite."

"All know Brod is heir!" the troll snarled.

"Of course," Sly said smoothly. "But no one will dare to challenge it as they did yesterday in the troll council."

Again the troll looked at Little Fur. "Brod has decided. Brod will present Little Fur to king as gift when king returns to Underth."

"What brilliance," Sly purred. "How clever and wise is Brod. How tricky and trollish."

The troll bellowed with laughter, then glanced at the fox's cage. "Pity fox not awake. Brod could make him scream to celebrate."

"Once the fox knows we have his mistress, that will be torment enough," Sly said viciously. "Let him wake to find her here."

The troll laughed again and reached down to scoop up Sly. He draped her about his neck, and as he turned and went toward the door of the chamber, Sly looked back at Little Fur. Her green eye glimmered as the door closed behind them.

"She betrayed you," said a new voice.

Little Fur smelled that the new voice was coming from a small cage under the one containing the fox, but she did not recognize its scent. "What are you?" Little Fur asked.

"I am a monkey," the creature replied. "I listened to the tale the fox told. The place he called a machine was a human experiment house. Many animals are kept in such places, though not all are as cruelly used as the fox. I myself was in such a place for a time, though I was not taken from my mother's body and put inside a machine as the fox was."

"How did you escape?"

The monkey gave a chittering laugh. "It was not difficult. Some humans smell of softness and sweetness and regret. I chose such a one to beguile, knowing that it would help me to be free. But before I could escape, the trolls carried me away."

"The trolls?" Little Fur could hardly believe what she was hearing.

"The Troll King is not a thick-headed fool like Brod. He is clever and subtle and patient. He has been studying humans for a long time, and there was something in that place that he wanted, a terrible sickness that humans had brewed. It was in a tiny glass bottle. A greep who had worked there when he was still human showed the Troll King where it was hidden, and he took it. Then the greep told the Troll King to take me, too, after it read the writing on my cage."

"Writing?" Little Fur wondered at the word.

"It is a thing that humans do. It means putting words down as marks that others can understand. The marks spoke to the greep, and he told the Troll King to take me, for my blood holds the antidote to the sickness in the glass bottle."

"Antidote?" Little Fur echoed. The word smelled like a potion to heal those poisoned by snake bite. She wanted to ask what the Troll King wanted with the sickness in a bottle, but she heard the sound of the door opening. Her heart began to beat very fast, but it was not Brod. There were a number of trolls, and they were carrying something. They set it down after a long and rather stupid argument about where it should be put, and then they went out again, leaving one troll behind to guard.

Little Fur did not want to think of Sly's betrayal. Sly had obviously told the trolls where to find her. But why had she gone to such lengths to convince the troll to leave hurting her to the Troll King? It must have also been Sly's doing that the troll guards had been warned to let her walk on her own two feet. Was Sly really saving Little Fur for the Troll King's pleasure? Little Fur found that she could not believe it. But what other reason could Sly have? Unless . . .

Unless Sly had not wanted Brod to hurt her or

cause her to be taken from the flow of earth magic! Little Fur thought of something else. She had believed Gazrak was the betrayer, and she had been wrong. Gazrak had proven loyal and courageous. Could she be wrong about Sly? She had asked Sly to help her get into the palace to find Sorrow, and that was what the cat had done. And now Sly had made sure no one would hurt her, for a while at least. Was it possible that she intended to help Little Fur and the fox to escape? Wasn't *that* what had been in her green eye as the troll had carried her away?

Little Fur was suddenly sure that she was right. Had not the earth spirit whispered to her to have faith? Perhaps this was what it had meant.

"I will trust her," she whispered to herself.

"Trust whom?" Sorrow asked.

Little Fur told him of Sly's apparent betrayal, whispering so that the troll by the door would not hear. The more she spoke, the more certain she became that Sly's actions only seemed to be so.

The Sett Owl had foreseen betrayal, but she had not known that Sly would be part of the quest. So perhaps she could not foresee that the betrayal was a ploy. It was the only thing that made sense. Little Fur now felt sure that Sly had a plan to help them get free. She told Sorrow that they must prepare themselves to be rescued.

"The cat did not strike me as the self-sacrificing type," the fox said with faint irony.

"She is not," Little Fur said. "But neither is she a traitor to her friends."

"I am no expert on friendship," the fox said. "In any case, I am dying, and will soon be free without her help. But I hope she will come, for your sake." His words smelled of pity.

Little Fur realized that she had never smelled such a sentiment in the fox before. She sniffed and let all of her healing skills guide her; to her amazement, his spirit smelled less sick. But what could possibly have mended it?

It came to her then—and it was a very strange thought—that the fox's spirit had begun to heal because he had *spoken* of the sorrow that consumed him. He had told his story to her, and darkness had flowed out of his spirit as he did so. She wanted to tell him this, but more trolls entered the chamber. Her cage was flung open, and she was pulled out roughly and her hands were bound behind her back. She dared not struggle, lest the trolls pick her up and throw her over their shoulders. Only as they turned and tugged the rope to make her walk did Little Fur see Sly sitting nearby, watching with an enigmatic green eye.

There was a great jostling as all of the trolls foolishly tried to push through the door at once. Little Fur took that moment to look back at Sly and whisper, "I know you have not betrayed me, Sly. You can't help me now, but please, free the fox and the other animals in this terrible place and help them to get away."

There was no time for more, and she was not even certain that the cat had heard her over the grunting and snarling of the trolls. Once again,

Little Fur walked through the bleak halls of the Troll King's palace, and then out the front gates and into the square, where Brod was in the midst of a speech before hundreds of assembled trolls.

". . . king will see how clever is Brod!" Brod was saying, and then he caught sight of Little Fur. A smile of triumph lifted his surly features, and he waved to the guards to bring her closer. "See, here is Little Fur, that king hates. How it will please king to see her stumbling before us as us come to welcome king back to his kingdom."

Little Fur ought to have been faint with fear, for the trolls roared their approval and pressed nearer, prodding and jeering at her. But she had noticed something that drove all else from her mind. Brod wore a cord about his neck with a green stone hanging from it, *just as she did*. Was it possible that he had been related to her mother?

As Brod began to walk and the mob crowded after him, Little Fur tried to be brave. But though she could feel earth magic flowing through the black stone upon which Underth was built, there was no moss to allow the earth spirit to whisper of hope.

They paraded through the city to a bridge of stone that Little Fur knew must be Lessbridge, for Kingsbridge began inside the palace. Brod led the way over it, still shouting his own praises. At the end, there were two paths: one led toward the black hills of stone and the road to the surface, while the other branched to the left and ran along the river. Brod took the left path, and soon they came to a wide opening in the cavern wall that Little Fur knew must be the beginning of the under-road.

Brod stopped and made another speech, standing in its gaping mouth, and Little Fur stood swaying with weariness and hunger and thirst.

At last, Brod signaled, and the trolls surged past him into the tunnel. Brod followed, reeking of triumph. But they had not been walking long when a low, blood-chilling growl filled the tunnel. Brod and the other trolls stopped, horror twisting their hideous features. The growling grew in volume until it became a roaring bellow.

Sly suddenly shrilled at Brod to run, run for his life. A pack of dogs was coming!

Little Fur had heard that trolls feared dogs,

but she had never believed it until she saw the effect of Sly's words. A wave of terror rippled over the frozen trolls. They turned and fled, lumbering blindly back toward Underth. The troll who held the rope securing Little Fur turned, jerking the rope so hard that she stumbled and fell. When the troll saw that she had fallen, it flung the rope down and ran.

In a flash, Sly was beside her. "There is a crack in the wall alongside us. Hide until help comes!" Then she was gone, crying out to the trolls to run before the dogs tore them to pieces!

Little Fur scrambled to her feet and let her troll blood lead her to the nearest crack. She pressed herself into it as deep as she could manage, and then she made herself still. She was so tired that despite the barking of the dogs and her terror, she dozed.

CHAPTER 16

A Surprising Rescue

Something pricked Little Fur's hand. She opened her eyes, and was astonished to see Crow.

"Shh," he said. "Sly said to waiting until trolls passing by again. She telling them dog pack came to rescue Little Fur. They will come past again in force with armor and weapons, chasing. Once they going past, we following."

"Following!" Little Fur gasped.

"They not looking back," Crow assured her. "We go along under-road only to crack leading up. Black dog showing Crow that wayfulness to

217

Underth." Little Fur stared at him, her mind reeling. Surely he did not mean that he had been shown a way to Underth by the black dog?

"Listening!" Crow scolded.

Little Fur obeyed, and heard the steady beat of trolls marching. When they appeared, they were marching fast and wearing grim expressions. They carried great stone clubs and spears and knives. She caught a glimpse of Brod, a whip in his hand, his face contorted with rage. By his side ran Sly. For one moment, her bright green eye darted a glance at Little Fur, who was stunned to see laughter in it. Then Sly was gone.

The trolls marched by for so long that Little Fur thought Brod must have mustered all of the trolls left in Underth to come after the dog pack. At last, the drumming of their feet grew distant.

Little Fur climbed from the crack, and Crow's sharp beak made short work of her bindings.

"Crow flying ahead. Little Fur coming quickly." Crow took to his wings before she could ask the questions clamoring at her. There was nothing to do but walk as he had bidden.

Little Fur was so preoccupied by the puzzle of the black dog that it took her some time to notice something was coming along quietly in the darkness behind her. She sniffed, but the smell of troll was too strong to make out what it was. She walked faster, wishing Crow would return so that she could ask him to fly back to see if anything was following them.

The whisper of sound grew closer, and she thought she heard the scrabble of claws on stone. Was it rats creeping after her?

Little Fur turned. Better to face whatever it was than to wait until it attacked her from behind. The soft sounds came closer, and this time, when she sniffed, she could hardly believe her nose.

"Sorrow!" she cried softly, and then she saw him, limping painfully along the tunnel.

"Ye were right about the cat," he whispered. "She came into the chamber and gnawed through the ropes of all the cages. Then she bade all the animals that had been freed to run as fast and far as they could. She said it would be a good diversion. She told me to seek ye on the underroad. I did not want to go," the fox rasped. "But even dying, my spirit will not let me be. Once she opened the cage, my spirit bade me: *Run! Escape! Be free!* I could not refuse it." He drew a few weary breaths. "In truth, I would rather die under the open sky with the sun or stars above me."

Little Fur heard the whisper of wings and turned to see Crow landing. He looked at the fox. "You smelling very bad."

The fox gave a soft laugh.

"Crow, how much farther until we reach the crack?" Little Fur asked, worried because the fox

could not move swiftly, and the more time that
passed, the greater the danger of discovery.

"Just ahead being horrible narrowness of

crack, which is beginning of wayness to surface,"
Crow said, having hopped and flapped to perch
on her shoulder. "Black dog is waiting there," he
added blithely. "Too narrow for her to coming.
She pushing out muzzle to do barking. Very
terrifying, eh?" he added smugly.

"The black dog showed Crow a way to
Underth that let him use his wings," Little Fur
told the fox. Sorrow made no response. Little
Fur turned to see that he was staggering with
exhaustion, his eyes blank and unfocused. She
helped him through the crack in the wall and
edged through after him, being careful not to
bump Crow, still perched on her shoulder. The
crack widened a little way in, and there the fox
collapsed.

"He smells of death," came the low, husky
voice of the black dog.

Little Fur looked to see the dog's eyes gleaming in the darkness. "I do not think he can walk
any farther," she said. "He is too weak."

"I will carry him," the black dog said. Little

Fur struggled to drag the fox's limp form to where the black dog had slunk down onto her belly. Then she pulled Sorrow as gently as she could onto the dog's broad, warm back. As she did so, she felt the slickness of blood on the dog's black fur.

"You are hurt," she said.

"The rock bit me when I tried to force my way out of the crack. But it was good that I did not go through, for the one-eyed cat said there would then be no trail for a troll to sniff out."

They set off, the black dog leading and Little Fur following with Crow perched on her shoulder.

"Why did you come down to Underth?" Little Fur asked the dog when they had stopped beside a trickle of water. Little Fur tried to dribble water into the fox's mouth, but it just ran out.

The black dog said, "Crow was waiting by the tunnel to Underth when I returned after the hunting humans had gone. He threatened to peck my eyes out if I tried to hurt you. I told him that I no longer wished to kill you. I wanted only to learn your secrets. The crow smelled the truth of my words, but he said that your secrets would soon be inside the bellies of trolls."

"I don't have any secrets," Little Fur said in bewilderment.

"This is not the time for speaking secrets," the black dog said.

"So tell me how you came to speak to Sly. . . ."

"Crow told me of the quest to Underth. I asked why Crow had not gone with you. He lamented long and wearyingly about dark, narrow tunnels where wings could not go. I told him of another way to Underth that was a narrow and dark way to begin with, but where soon he could use his wings."

Crow took up the story. "Once we coming to crack opening, Crow flying into caverns of Underth. Flying high and quiet in shadows like bat! Crow having eyesight of eagle! Seeing Sly. Crow flying to talk with black cat. Telling of courageous and dangerous journey to Underth with black dog. Sly telling that Little Fur captivated by trolls! Sly saying trolls fearing dogs. She telling that she having plan to saving Little Fur. Crow leading her to crack, and black cat talking to black dog."

"We should go on," the black dog said.

Little Fur nodded and pulled the fox onto the dog's back again, whispering to his limp form that it was not far before they would come to the sky, hoping it was true. Her elf blood was waking and yearning for blue sky and sunlight too.

At last they came into the road serpents' tunnel. It was a different place than before, but Little Fur could smell that they were not far from another of the beast feeding caverns. The black dog padded along the tracks toward the smell. Little Fur followed warily, and stopped at the sight of the blaze of false light. A road serpent was being tended, but to her intense relief, she saw that they were approaching the back of the creature, so there was no danger.

Little Fur expected the dog to lead them to

another crack, but she continued to the feeding place. She stopped at the very rear of the road serpent just as it gave its rending cry and began to slide away along the rails. Then Little Fur saw that she meant to mount some steps that led up to the feeding platform.

"We cannot go up there," Little Fur said. "Humans will see us, and I cannot go where the earth magic does not flow."

"Have no fear," the black dog answered. "Crow will distract the humans as he did when we came this way before; there are places where the magic flows for you to touch."

"Do not fearing," Crow cawed, his beak tickling her ear. Then he launched himself, screaming and cawing, into the air.

To Little Fur's amazement, out of the shadows, as if they had waited for Crow's signal, poured a great cloud of chittering bats, their leathery wings rustling like leaves in a storm. Humans screamed and shouted and ran, and the smell of their terror was overwhelming. In moments,

there was not a human in sight. Little Fur was astonished that little blind peeping bats, with their gentle inquisitive natures, could give rise to such fear. Truly, humans were strange.

"Come," said the black dog.

Little Fur followed her up the steps. She was reassured to feel that earth magic flowed through them, for they were cut into living rock. At the top, she saw an astonishing thing. A set of gleaming silver steps rose swiftly as a flying bird toward the surface of the world.

"There is no earth magic in the metal of the moving steps, but the wall is true rock and it flows there. All you need do is touch it," the black dog told her.

Then she stepped onto the moving stairs and was carried upward. Little Fur might not have had the courage to follow, except that she saw the fox was slipping again. So she took a deep breath, reached out to the wall, and stepped onto the metal stairs. Keeping one hand against the stone wall, she mounted the steps on shaking legs until she could reach out her free hand to steady the fox. Thus they rose through the layers of earth as swiftly as Crow and the cloud of gleeful bats.

The stairs stopped, vanishing mysteriously into the ground. The companions found themselves in another great hall. Again the bats wheeled and swooped with Crow over the heads of the few humans. In minutes, the big space was empty.

"Come. Keep your hand on the wall," the black dog cautioned.

They passed along the one living wall in that great human cavern and entered another tunnel. It was short, and to Little Fur's delight, she felt the sweetness of wind laden with the heady scents of green and growing things.

And then they were outside!

The rock wall ended in a patch of green grass under a tree with low branches dense enough to provide some cover. Not that there were any humans about. Little Fur stopped, dizzy with the pleasure that ran through her at feeling green grass beneath her feet. She would have reached out to greet the tree, but her eyes came to rest on the fox and her elation faded.

"We should lay him down and let him die with the earth magic flowing under him," the black dog suggested in her deep, rumbling voice.

CHAPTER 17
The End of Sorrow

Little Fur knew that the black dog was right, yet she could not bring herself to lay Sorrow down and let him die by the side of a foul-smelling black road, within scent and sight of the humans who had done so much hurt to him. She would have liked to take him to her own beloved wilderness and lay him among the roots of the Old Ones, where he might have their comfort as he waited to join the world's dream. She had no hope of healing him now, not even there, where the flow of earth magic was so strong. That he had not died already was the doing of his spirit, which even now fought to hold him to life.

"I would take him to the beaked house," Little Fur said to the black dog, blinking back tears.

"Very well," the black dog said. "But he might not live long enough to arrive."

Little Fur shook her head, unable to speak. She could hardly bear it that having gone through so much, the fox would die just when his spirit had begun to heal. The black dog went on, and Little Fur followed, sensing that Crow was flying overhead and would warn them of any approaching human.

Little Fur found herself deeply confused by the mingling of newly strengthened troll blood with her reawakened elf blood. So compelling was the conflict between her two bloods that it seemed only a moment before they were within sight of the beaked house. By then, Little Fur's troll blood had again given way to her elf blood.

The dog carried the fox to the tree that grew by the far side of the beaked house. Little Fur carefully eased him down onto the thickly fallen leaves. She had not dared to use her senses, fearing that he must be dead, but when she laid her hands on him, she found that he lived yet.

Little Fur lifted his head gently onto her knees, wondering why this one death filled her with such terrible sadness. All things died and came to the world's dream in their own time, and she did not fear death for herself or any creature. Perhaps it was the story the fox had told in the troll cavern, of a life that had been stolen before it could be lived, but it seemed to Little Fur that the fox's death would be a terrible wrong. She plucked some dew-drenched leaves and wiped them over Sorrow's swollen tongue.

The flutter of feathers overhead made her look up, expecting to see Crow alighting. But to her amazement, it was the Sett Owl. The old bird landed in the tree and looked down at the fox. "He is dying. That is a pity."

"You promised it to him," Little Fur said sadly.

"I had hoped that he would not want that promise kept. But you have helped him."

"His spirit is no longer sick, but his body . . ."

"Yes, there is a point beyond which a body cannot be healed," the owl said with a sigh.

"Do you know what happened in Underth?" Little Fur asked.

"I have seen much of it in visions, and I do not need to know all things at this time."

"Do you know if Sly is all right, and Ginger and the ferrets? And Gazrak? Gazrak . . ."

"I know what Gazrak did, and I am glad of it for his sake. As to my worthy servant and his companions, they make the slow journey here."

A ferret appeared, and he was so much like Shikra and Brave Kell that Little Fur knew he must be a relative. Like them, he carried a little pack of food and a bowl of water.

"This is a brother of Shikra and Kell," said the Sett Owl. "When I foresaw your coming, I asked the ferrets to prepare such food and herbs as would nourish you and ease the fox. I had hoped that Sorrow might be saved, but I think perhaps it is better not to trouble him."

Little Fur looked at Sorrow and knew the owl was right, yet she decided she would clean the wounds. She opened the pack and forgot all else but her healing.

❊   ❊   ❊

Hours later, her back hurt, and she could tell from the light that it was almost noon. The Sett Owl suggested kindly that she rest.

"I have done all I can for him," Little Fur told her. "I know it is silly when he is so near to dying, but it seemed . . . proper."

"No wonder the Troll King fears you," the Sett Owl said, and her voice was warm.

Little Fur sighed. "I am sorry we did not learn the Troll King's plan. It has something to do with a creature called an indyk and with a bottle of sickness stolen from humans. . . ."

"Indyk is not a creature but a name," a swift, light voice interrupted. Little Fur looked around and saw a small, dark-furred creature only slightly bigger than Crow sitting on the grass. She recognized the smell. "You are the monkey from the cage under Sorrow. You told me about the human experiment houses."

"Indyk is my name," the small beast said. "Your one-eyed cat friend set me free. In return, I will tell you the Troll King's plan. It is only a little more of the tale I told you already. The humans created the sickness in the bottle to hurt other humans. It came from a place where many such things are made. Weapons, humans call them. The sickness the Troll King stole was a weapon."

"I don't understand," Little Fur said.

"The sickness causes a rage of madness and violence. And once a single human is infected, the sickness will leap on their breaths to thousands of other humans. It may be that all humans catch the sickness and would open many other glass bottles which contain far worse weapons—things that will ravage the earth and kill the earth spirit."

"The cat sickness?"

"The greep made it to prove to the Troll King how easily a sickness can be used against an enemy," the monkey said.

"What will happen now?" Little Fur asked.

"Nothing." The monkey chittered with laughter. "How would the Troll King dare use a sickness when he does not have me and my blood to make an antidote? For the sickness can be caught by trolls as well as humans."

"He will be angry," Little Fur said. She looked at the Sett Owl. "He will guess that you sent me."

"Do not fear for either of us," the owl said. "Brod is even now telling his master that Little Fur came with a pack of dogs to Underth to steal his precious antidote and spy on him in his very own city. The Troll King will fear Little Fur even more than he hates her after this, and he will not quickly plot harm against her and her friends for fear of what she will do to him."

"What about the humans who made the sickness in the bottle?"

"They will learn fear when they discover that

not only is the bottle missing, but also the monkey whose blood contains the only means of making a cure. If they dare to admit the loss to their masters, the place where it was made will be closed."

The owl turned her enormous fierce eyes to the monkey, who was watching her with lively curiosity. "You will need a place to stay, Indyk, for soon it will be winter. The beaked house is a pleasant place to live, and I would like to hear all that you observed while with the humans and when you were a captive in Underth."

"That is kind of you," Indyk said simply.

The owl flapped down to the ground. "I will go back into the beaked house now. I cannot fly up easily, and so I must waddle like a duck through the tunnel and save my strength for the flight back up to my roost." She looked again at the fox, who had not stirred. "There is no need for you to stay if you wish to return to the wilderness of the Old Ones, Little Fur. The earth magic will allow nothing to interfere with one who fought so valiantly for it."

"I will stay until the end," Little Fur said softly.

Left alone, the healer gazed into the ravaged face of the fox and ran her fingers gently over his black-streaked pelt, feeling the many scars left by the human that Sorrow had thought a brother.

Clouds gathered and made the day dull. After a time, the two black-robed humans that looked after the beaked house arrived. Little Fur's heart beat faster at the sight of them, but neither of them even looked toward the tree where she sat with the dying fox.

After the two humans departed, a fitful wind blew up, rustling the leaves on the cobbles and making the dust hiss. The ferret brought more water and herbs and a sweet nut mash. Little Fur mixed salves and potions and applied them, unable to sit and let the fox die. She wondered how long the fox's spirit would hold his body to life.

Looking up at the tree arching its branches over her, Little Fur began to sing to it the song of their journey. She wanted the earth spirit to know how she felt about Sorrow's story. She sent her song deep, so that the earth spirit should know who its true warrior had been.

Night shadows were forming under the tree and about the edges of the beaked house when Little Fur noticed the black dog was sitting a little way off by the spiked fence, watching her.

"I have not had the chance to properly thank you for helping the fox," Little Fur said.

The black dog came closer. "You love him," she said in her expressionless tone.

Little Fur realized that it was true. "I wish I could have helped him. You asked about my secrets. If there are any secrets I have that you want, I am happy to share them."

"I wish to know the secret of your power," said the black dog.

"My power?" Little Fur echoed.

"I wish to understand the power with which you stopped me from killing you. How did you know what words to say?" the dog asked.

Little Fur struggled to recall what she had said. It seemed very long ago. Then she remembered. She had told Ginger and Sorrow not to hurt the black dog. The dog had asked why she had stopped them, and she had stammered that she was a healer. That was all. "I don't understand what you mean."

"My human masters taught me about the power of muscle and bone and teeth. They pitted me against other dogs and I won and won. I gloried in my strength. But I was not content. It seemed to me that if I could become strong enough, I would find peace, but peace never came, and in the end, I was half mad with rage. That madness caused me to break my bonds to seek out the cat and you. But when you spoke, all rage leaked out of me. Now I want only to understand the secret of the words that disarmed me."

"I don't know how to teach you words," Little Fur said slowly. "But if you want to come to the wilderness with me and see what I do there, you are welcome."

The dog thanked her gravely and then went away, saying she would seek her out soon in the wilderness.

Little Fur watched her go, a great dark lump of a creature with no name, and wondered what Tillet would say when the dog appeared. The wilderness would already know from the tree on whose roots she sat that Little Fur had invited her.

She looked up and watched the sky darken and stars prick the blackness, and the bond she shared with Ginger told her that the gray cat was somewhere far away, also gazing at the stars, and thinking of her. *I love him, too,* she thought, *and he loves me.*

The moon had just risen when Indyk came and peered for a moment at the fox before going inside the beaked house.

Little Fur looked down and was startled to see the fox's eyes were open.

"Little Fur," he whispered.

She held him close and stroked his soft ears. "I am here, Sorrow. See where we are, under the tree beside the beaked house? We got back safely, and we did what we swore to do. We know what the Troll King planned. . . ."

"I heard ye singing," Sorrow murmured. Suddenly Little Fur realized that he no longer radiated that sickly heat. She loosed her healing senses that she had kept tightly furled, not wanting to feel each second of the fox's dying. The infection in his wounds was still deep and dangerous. But it had eased. Hardly daring to breathe, Little Fur pressed her senses deeper

until she felt it: Sorrow's spirit. It blazed within him like a star, making her catch her breath, for she had never encountered such a force. It was ragged and battered and yet as lovely as starlight on water or dew on a cobweb, as lovely as the song of the Old Ones.

Suddenly Little Fur knew that the fox's warrior spirit had no intention of letting the wounds to his body kill him.

Sorrow was going to live!

ACKNOWLEDGMENTS

Thanks to Nan McNab, who received *Sorrow* in various degrees of chaos and tended its flesh and spirit with Little Fur's own sweet grace; to Jan and Jiří Tibor Novák, for inspiration and advice; to Peter Cross, who remains an unstinting source of creative friendship; to my brother Ken, who lends me his precious art books even when he knows it will take forever to get them back; and especially to the wonderful Marina Messiha, for her beautiful, tender design of the Little Fur series.

LITTLE FUR'S TRIALS AND
TRIUMPHS CONTINUE IN:

Book 3: A Mystery of Wolves
Book 4: A Riddle of Green

COMING SOON!

ABOUT THE AUTHOR

Isobelle Carmody began the first of her highly acclaimed Obernewtyn Chronicles while she was still in high school, and worked on it while completing a bachelor of arts and then a journalism cadetship. The series and her short stories have established her at the forefront of fantasy writing in Australia.

She has written many award-winning short stories and books for young people. *The Gathering* was a joint winner of the 1993 CBC Book of the Year Award and the 1994 Children's Peace Literature Award. *Billy Thunder and the Night Gate* (published as *Night Gate* in the United States) was short-listed for the Patricia Wrightson Prize for Children's Literature in the 2001 NSW Premier's Literary Awards.

Isobelle divides her time between her homes in Australia and the Czech Republic.